## STEELE ENTERPRISES, INC.
### MEMO

TO: Note to self
FROM: Jonathan Steele, CEO

• Check on Cynthia Morgan's progress at Vanderbilt Hospital—looks quite hopeful!

• Follow up with police—must find out who would poison such a sweet, beautiful woman.

• Set up nursery at home for baby nephew.

• Consider Cynthia's offer as temporary nanny—though must beware of those sparks flying between us...

Dear Reader,

As the Intimate Moments quarter of our yearlong 20th anniversary promotion draws to a close, we offer you a month so full of reading excitement, you'll hardly know where to start. How about with *Night Shield*, the newest NIGHT TALES title from *New York Times* bestselling author Nora Roberts? As always, Nora delivers characters you'll never forget and a plot guaranteed to keep you turning the pages. And don't miss our special NIGHT TALES reissue, also available this month wherever you buy books.

What next? How about *Night of No Return*, rising star Eileen Wilks's contribution to our in-line continuity, A YEAR OF LOVING DANGEROUSLY? This emotional and suspenseful tale will have you on the edge of your seat—and longing for the next book in the series. As an additional treat this month, we offer you an in-line continuation of our extremely popular out-of-series continuity, 36 HOURS. Bestselling author Susan Mallery kicks things off with *Cinderella for a Night*. You'll love this book, along with the three Intimate Moments novels—and one stand-alone Christmas anthology—that follow it.

Rounding out the month, we have a new book from Beverly Bird, one of the authors who helped define Intimate Moments in its very first month of publication. She's joined by Mary McBride and Virginia Kantra, each of whom contributes a top-notch novel to the month.

Next month, look for a special two-in-one volume by Maggie Shayne and Marilyn Pappano, called *Who Do You Love?* And in November, watch for the debut of our stunning new cover design.

Leslie J. Wainger
Executive Senior Editor

Please address questions and book requests to:
Silhouette Reader Service
U.S.: 3010 Walden Ave., P.O. Box 1325, Buffalo, NY 14269
Canadian: P.O. Box 609, Fort Erie, Ont. L2A 5X3

# CINDERELLA FOR A NIGHT
## SUSAN MALLERY

Silhouette®

INTIMATE™MOMENTS®

Published by Silhouette Books

America's Publisher of Contemporary Romance

Special thanks and acknowledgment
are given to Susan Mallery for her contribution
to the 36 Hours series.

SILHOUETTE BOOKS

ISBN 0-373-27099-2

CINDERELLA FOR A NIGHT

Visit Silhouette at www.eHarlequin.com

**Printed in U.S.A.**

**Books by Susan Mallery**

## SUSAN MALLERY

is the bestselling author of over thirty books for Silhouette. Always a fan of romance novels, Susan finds herself in the unique position of living out her own personal romantic fantasy with the new man in her life. Susan lives in sunny Southern California with her handsome hero husband and her two adorable-but-not-bright cats.

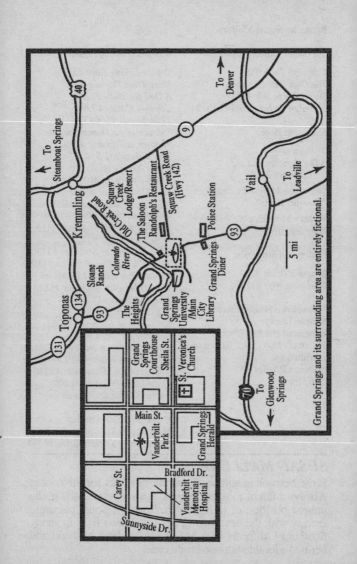

Grand Springs and its surrounding area are entirely fictional.

# Chapter 1

"You look like Cinderella," thirteen-year-old Jenny Morgan breathed as she stared at her older sister in the mirror.

"You're right," Cynthia Morgan said with a laugh. "All I need now are the mice!" She spread out the full skirt of the rented aqua-colored ball gown and gently swayed back and forth. "A handsome prince would be nice, too."

"You'll find him," Jenny said confidently. "He'll take one look at you and fall madly in love."

"A girl can hope."

But Cynthia wasn't expecting much in the way of handsome princes at the Grand Springs Charity Masquerade Halloween Ball. For one thing, Grand Springs, Colorado, wasn't a hangout for the handsome prince set. For another thing, she wasn't princess material. Tonight, in her rented ball gown, with her hair pulled up and wearing more makeup than usual, highlighting her pleasant if not spectacular features, she looked pretty good. But the charity event attracted Grand Springs social elite and "pretty good" was not going to put her in the running for anyone very special. Certainly not for Jonathan Steele, a living breathing Prince Charming if there ever was one.

"Let me look."

Cynthia turned at the sound of her mother's voice and smiled as Betsy Morgan's face softened into an expression of maternal pride.

"You're a vision," Betsy announced.

"*I* said she looked like Cinderella."

"You know what?" Cynthia asked as she leaned forward and kissed her mother's cheek. "I think I'm the luckiest person in world because I have a wonderful, supportive family and I get to go to a swishy ball tonight at the Grand Springs Empress Hotel. I promise I'll memorize details and tell you both everything in the morning."

Betsy exchanged a conspiratorial look with Jenny. "Not so fast." She disappeared into the hallway, then reappeared carrying a shoebox. "We have a surprise for you."

Cynthia stared at the box, then looked at both her mother and sister. "Tell me you didn't."

Jenny beamed. "We did. We voted and even Brad and Brett agreed and they're exactly the right color and you'll look so pretty when you're dancing." She crossed her arms over her chest and tightly squeezed herself. "When I grow up I want to be exactly like you, Cynthia. I want to go to a Halloween ball and be beautiful."

Cynthia turned to her mother. "Are you sure about this? It's just for one night."

Betsy shrugged. "Sometimes that's all you need to find a little magic in your life. You've been so good to all of us. We wanted to give something back." She laughed. "Besides, they're just shoes."

They were more than that and Cynthia knew it. Money was tight in the Morgan household. Cynthia had used up the last of her pitiful savings to rent her finery for the evening. While the princess costume came complete with a tiara and fake jewelry, it hadn't included matching shoes. She'd seen a pair of dyeable pumps on sale a week ago, but hadn't had the money. Her mother had offered the household's "what if" fund—a jar full of change that everyone contributed to. The rule was each member of the family had an equal vote on how the money was spent. Generally it went for a fun dinner out or an evening at a local arcade.

"I can't believe you all wanted me to have these shoes," she said and opened the lid.

Inside were a pair of aqua pumps that matched her rented dress perfectly. She slipped them on, then stood in front of the mirror while her mother and sister fussed over her. All of the Morgan kids were blond and fair. With the exception of Cynthia, they had big blue eyes inherited from their mother. Jenny was still too skinny and had a mouthful of braces, but in a couple of years she would be as pretty as Betsy. The ten-year-old twins—Brad and Brett—took more after their father and would grow to tower over the women in the family.

"Are you ready?" Betsy asked after smoothing the hem of the dress. "You look amazing."

Cynthia met her gaze in the mirror and smiled. The rented dress smelled faintly of mothballs and her long, elbow-length gloves had been bought at a thrift store and mended. The tiara was rhinestones, the pearls around her neck fake, but for tonight none of that mattered.

"I feel great," Cynthia told her and picked up her small handbag. "So if I stay out past midnight, will my car turn into a pumpkin?"

Betsy and Jenny followed her to the front door. "Not possible. It's already a wreck," her mother said cheerfully. "Pumpkin would be an improvement."

Cynthia kissed Jenny's cheek then her mother's, and walked toward her battered car. "You're right. Don't wait up, Mom. I'll be fine."

"Promise me you'll dance at least once with the most handsome man there," Betsy called out as her daughter started her ugly but reliable car.

"I'll do my best."

She waved at her sister and her mother, then shifted into gear and started down the driveway. A shiver of anticipation rippled through her. For the first time in her life she was going to see how the other half lived. More important, she was actually going to speak to Jonathan Steele. At least that was her plan.

"I can do it, I can do it," she chanted quietly to herself as she drove through the dark streets of Grand Springs. The mountain evening was cool and a starlit sky twinkled overhead. A magical night, she thought cheerfully. The kind of night where anything could happen. Meeting the great Jonathan Steele was the main reason she'd been so excited by the opportunity to attend the charity ball.

Two years ago she'd received a grant of seed money to start her new business. Now a relatively flourishing concern, Mother's Helper existed because of Jonathan Steele's generosity. The billionaire gave back to the community on a regular basis. He provided start-up capital for dozens of fledgling concerns. He was also the sponsor of the night's charity ball.

"I will go up to him and, in a poised and confident manner, thank him. I will be gracious and brief and I will not trip or fall or forget to talk or anything else humiliating."

Cynthia had a brief image of herself spilling punch down the front of his tailored, expensive tux and made a mental note not to be carrying anything liquid when she made her way to his side.

"Maybe we'll dance," she said dreamily, wondering what it would be like to be in Jonathan's strong arms. He was so very handsome. Tall and dark and...

"And completely out of my league," she reminded herself as she approached the well-lit Grand Springs Empress Hotel. Jonathan was a tycoon who dated incredibly beautiful, glamorous women. She was a struggling owner of a company that provided temporary live-in nanny care. If she was very lucky, she just might get to thank him, but that was it.

She paused at the crest of the rise to admire the twinkling lights of the hotel, glittering like a wedding cake in the rugged, rustic setting. The looming mountains were dark shadows in the distance. She breathed in the crisp night air and drove onto the hotel grounds.

She pulled up to the valet who took one look at her car and visibly shuddered. Cynthia glanced at the luxury car in front of her, then shrugged.

"My other car is much nicer," she teased as she stepped out and accepted the parking ticket. "With this one I don't have to worry about it being stolen."

The valet, a young man about her age, relaxed enough to grin. "Like I believe that. Don't worry, I've parked worse." He jerked his head toward the open glass doors. "The ballroom is on your left. Have a nice evening."

"I will," she promised, speaking to both herself and to him.

Squaring her shoulders, she clutched her small, cloth bag in one hand and stepped forward, prepared to meet her destiny.

Jonathan Steele accepted a glass of champagne from a passing waiter's tray, then took a sip. He eyed the mingling crowd filling the oversize room and knew that it had been a mistake for him to come tonight. He wasn't in the mood to play the game of gracious host. He hated events like these. Too many business acquaintances presumed on a relationship that didn't exist. Too many women thought it was well past time he was married. Debutantes and their persistent mothers cornered him at every turn and more married women than he could count thought he would be a fun, if temporary, companion.

But convention demanded that he make an appearance, so he was here. As soon as he was able, he would make his escape and retreat to the solitude that was more comfortable, if not more preferred.

He took a second sip of champagne only to have the fizzy liquid choke him when he spotted a familiar couple across the room. Anger burned through him—a molten rage that made his fingers tighten dangerously on the delicate crystal.

Jonathan set down his glass on a nearby table, then walked through the crowd. His gaze never left the darkly handsome pair talking with friends. The man was tall, nearly his own height. The wife, a too-thin former model in a clinging black gown, had a haughty look about her pinched features.

He stopped beside his half brother and tapped David on the shoulder. "I would like a word with you," he said.

David turned slowly, his expression unconcerned. "Jonathan, what a pleasure. But then you're the sponsor of tonight's ball, so I suppose it isn't a surprise that you're here."

David Steele, younger by seven years, had lived the good life since the day he was born. He didn't know what it was to build something, to work hard and be proud of his accomplishments. Instead he expected all things would come to him and much to Jonathan's disgust, they generally did. But that was about to change.

"Excuse me, darling," David said, lightly kissing his wife's cheek. "I'll be right with you."

Lisa Steele offered her brother-in-law a cold smile. "Don't keep him for too long, Jonathan. I'm lost without him."

"I'm sure that's true," Jonathan said smoothly, wondering how Lisa and her husband would maintain their marriage when they were in prison.

Jonathan took David's arm and led him to a private alcove in the large ballroom. The two men were both over six feet, each with a strong build. Their gazes locked.

"The game's up," Jonathan said bluntly. "I've known about your embezzling for months, but now I have proof. Either put the money back or I'll inform the authorities in the morning."

David smiled slowly. "You don't have proof. You don't have anything. This is a bluff."

Jonathan's gaze narrowed. "I never bluff. You know

that. It would give me great pleasure to see you arrested for this, David. Don't push me."

Jonathan didn't know why he was giving his brother time. He should call in the police right now. But he knew he wouldn't.

David raised his dark eyebrows. "You think you have it all planned out, big brother, but you don't. This time I'm going to win. You see, Lisa and I are going away. You won't be able to find us. In a very short period of time, you'll have an unfortunate but fatal accident. Lisa and I can return as the grieving family. You'll be gone and we'll have everything." He waved his hand like a wand. "Presto—I win."

Coldness filled Jonathan's chest. He hadn't known it could get any worse between himself and his brother. He'd thought the truly low point of their relationship had been when their father had left David the family home. It had been the only thing Jonathan had ever wanted, but the elder Steele had intended to send a message from the grave. David had waited just long enough for the title to clear in his name, then he'd offered it to Jonathan at twice its value.

The house had been Jonathan's only link with his past. He would have paid more to take possession and he'd given his brother the money.

Now David was threatening to have him killed. He almost didn't believe they were having this conversation. "Why?" he asked.

"Why am I stealing or why do I want you eliminated?"

Jonathan shrugged. "Either. Both."

"I would think the reason I want you gone is obvious. Father left you the firm, but I'm the heir when you're dead. Now I'll take it from you."

Jonathan didn't doubt his brother's desire to have what he, Jonathan, had built. David had always been greedy. "If you're planning to kill me, why embezzle?"

David leaned close and lowered his voice to a whisper. Unholy pleasure glinted in his eyes. "Because I can. Because it hurts you. I'll miss causing you pain when you're dead. It's my favorite hobby. Oh, well. I'll find another."

With that, David slapped him on the back and walked away. Jonathan watched him go. From the moment David had been born thirty years ago, he'd been the golden boy of the family. Jonathan had never understood why. David had been given every opportunity, but he'd wasted them all. He took what he wanted and when he was tired of it, he destroyed it.

Jonathan thought about his brother's threat to his life. He didn't doubt that David had a plan. And just as soon as Jonathan left the party, he would call the detective he'd been working with and pass along the information. No doubt he would be told to hire a bodyguard or lie low for a few days.

He waited for a sense of outrage or anger, but he was tired of it all. There wasn't anything left for him to feel. He'd been trying to understand his brother for too long, just as he'd been trying to get their father's attention. It didn't matter that Jonathan had taken a failing division of Steele Enterprises and had turned it into a multibillion-dollar success. His father had barely noticed.

Years before, Jonathan had decided that families were an invention of the devil and nothing had happened since to change his mind. He didn't want to have to put his only living relative in prison, but David wasn't going to give him a choice.

He swore and stepped out of the alcove. The laughter

and loud conversation in the room seemed to echo in his head. He decided it was time to go home. If David really planned to kill him, he didn't want his last night to be spent here.

He turned to leave, only to collide into a cloud of aqua silk and tulle. A young woman took a step back, then looked at him and smiled.

"You know, I had an entire conversation with myself on the way over here in which I swore I was not going to spill wine on anyone." She looked down at the puddle on the floor, then returned her attention to his jacket. "Did I get you or miss you?"

He was sure he'd seen every debutante in the county and most of those in the state. He had a great memory for faces and knew instantly he hadn't met this young woman before.

She was of average height, with pale skin and hazel-green eyes. She wore her blond hair up in a simple style, anchored by a ridiculous tiara. There was an air of innocence about her. If this had been another time and place, he would have sworn she was a vicar's daughter in from the country for the first time in her life.

He touched the hem of his jacket. It was dry. "You missed me."

She pressed a hand to her chest. "Thank goodness. I would have hated to soak you." She waved her now-empty glass. "At least it was white wine. That doesn't stain, does it?" She bit her lower lip and blushed slightly. "I'm babbling. It's horrible, but you make me nervous. I mean, you're *you* and I'm not. Well, I mean of course I'm not you. And spilling, it's just so high school. Don't you hate that?"

She paused for breath. "You're not in costume."

He glanced down at his dark tuxedo. "I know." His

gaze returned to her. He took in the ball gown, the tiara, the wonder in her eyes. "You must be Cinderella."

"Almost. Cynthia." She bit her lower lip again. "Please don't call me Cindy. It would be too embarrassing." She gave him a shy smile. "And you're Jonathan Steele. I recognize you from your pictures in the newspaper. You look better in color than in black and white."

"How reassuring."

She glanced around, then back at him. "People stare at you. Have you noticed? I can't decide if it's because you're good-looking or if it's the money-power thing. Do you know which it is? Or is it both?"

The complete lack of guile in her eyes told him that her question was genuine, not an attempt at flattery.

"Maybe it's you," he told her.

She waved her hand in a gesture of dismissal. "Oh, please. There's a laugh. You're the king of the ball."

"You're in a tiara. You must be royalty as well."

She grinned. "Sure. I'm the Princess of Nowhere." She set her glass on a nearby tray then curtsied. "It's a small kingdom on the edge of town. Perhaps you've heard of it?"

Jonathan had spent the past two months confirming that his only living relative had concocted a scheme to skim millions from his business. That same relative had just informed him that he had arranged for his murder. If David didn't put the money back, which was unlikely, Jonathan was going to have to have him arrested. It had been a hell of day.

Yet despite that, he suddenly didn't want to leave the ball. His house was a cold, empty place and the past echoed through the many rooms. Instead he found himself wanting to be with the mysterious Cynthia—perhaps the last innocent on the planet. He wanted to hear her views on things like the best flavors of ice cream and who else had she spilled drinks on that evening and did he really make her nervous.

The orchestra in the corner started a waltz. Jonathan bowed formally. "May I have this dance, Your Highness?"

Cynthia smiled and held out her arms. "Okay, but I have to warn you the kingdom didn't have money for a dance instructor so your toes are in danger. Just don't try anything wild and I'll probably be able to stumble along."

He drew her close, enjoying the feel of her curvy body against his hard, male planes. Up close her fake finery lost some of its glitter, but he found he didn't mind. She was, he decided, a genuine person, and he couldn't remember the last time he'd had the pleasure of dancing with one.

This wasn't really happening, Cynthia thought as Jonathan swept her around the room. It was all she could do to hold back her squeals of delight. For the first time in her life, her dreams were coming true.

She'd been wishing and hoping that she might have a chance to speak with Jonathan Steele and thank him for all he'd unknowingly done for her. But now she was in his arms and dancing with him. Her heart pounded so hard in her chest, she thought she might be in danger of swooning.

"Tell me about life in your kingdom," Jonathan said as they twirled past other couples in the rapidly spinning ballroom. "Is there a prince in your life?"

She wasn't sure if he was teasing or not. "I'm not married, if that's what you're asking."

A slow, male smile tugged at the corners of his mouth. He had a wonderful mouth, she thought dreamily as she inhaled his masculine scent. Firm, almost stern looking, and studying it made her wonder how it would feel against her own. He was tall, too, and the faint whispers of silver at his temples were so intriguing. She wasn't sure how old he was. Several years older than herself, which meant he was probably wildly experienced with women and she was making a fool of herself with him, but she couldn't find the will to mind very much.

"That's exactly what I wanted to know." His dark eyes glittered with a light she couldn't recall seeing in a man's eyes before. Not that she'd had much experience with being this close to men like Jonathan Steele.

They continued to dance, moving easily, as if they'd whirled around the floor a thousand times before. She found herself pressing against him, her breasts flattening against his broad chest, her legs brushing his through the yards of tulle and silk of her ball gown.

"So why haven't I seen you before?" he asked. "Are you new in town?"

Cynthia laughed. "I've lived here all my life. We don't exactly travel in the same circles."

"But I thought all the royals knew each other."

He was teasing her. She couldn't believe it. She didn't know that men like him knew how to tease. "I guess you missed me, then."

"I guess I did. I'm glad I've had the chance to fix my mistake."

His gaze locked with hers. She could feel the shiver rippling through her body, making her legs weak and her heart flutter like a trapped bird. She was going to faint or start laughing hysterically, or throw herself at

his feet and beg him to do whatever it was men like
him did to young women like herself.

"Aren't you going to tell me about yourself?" he
asked.

"There's not much to tell," she said. "I work for—"

"Let me guess," he said, cutting her off. He drew
her to the edge of the dance floor, then slowed to a stop.
"You teach kindergarten, or first grade. You have
something to do with small children."

Her eyes widened. "How did you know?"

"You have that look about you."

"What look?"

"The look of an innocent." He reached up and
touched her cheek. "I can't remember the last time I
met someone like you, Princess Cynthia. I can't decide
if you're Cinderella or the Princess of Nowhere. What
happens at midnight? Do you disappear and leave me
with only your shoe?"

She didn't know how to answer. His fingers were a
light caress that she felt all the way down to her toes
curling in her new shoes. Goose bumps erupted on her
arms and her breath caught in her throat. She and Jonathan were playing a very grown-up game and she
didn't have enough experience to understand the rules.
If there were any rules. Maybe people made them up
as they went along.

"I don't have to disappear," she whispered. Heat
flared on her cheeks and she ducked her head to hide
her blush.

He swore. "Don't do that," he told her even as he
took her hand and led her into an alcove of the ballroom. One minute they were in the middle of the crowd,
the next they were in a private paradise, tucked between
a row of plants and a curtained wall.

"Don't do what?"

"Blush. If you blush it means I can't do what I want."

She risked glancing at him. "What do you want to do?"

She asked the question with no expectation of an answer, but as soon as the words fell from her lips, she knew exactly what he wanted to do…or she had a pretty good idea.

"Find out what innocence tastes like," he said, and gently cupped her face. Then he lowered his head and brushed his mouth against her lips.

She hadn't been sure what to expect. If someone had asked her to guess about Jonathan Steele's kissing technique, she would have said that the man probably took what he wanted. But this wasn't like that at all. His touch was gentle, tender, almost asking, as if he wanted to be sure that she was fully aware of what was going on and that she liked it.

What was there not to like, she thought hazily as tiny explosions seemed to go off inside her entire body. Fire rushed through her, as if every inch of her had just had a close encounter with a major heat source. His fingers branded her, his lips teased and she knew that if she died this very moment, it would be with the knowledge that she'd experienced something incredibly perfect.

They weren't touching anywhere but their mouths. Yet it was as if he pressed into her. She sensed his nearness and it was an intoxicating presence. His lips, moved against hers…slowly, lightly but with a thoroughness that left every millimeter of her mouth caressed and aroused. His breath fanned her face. She thought briefly of opening her eyes, but her eyelids were too heavy. Besides, she didn't want to destroy the perfection of the kiss.

He turned his head slightly, then brushed his tongue against her lower lip. She shivered and parted for him. For a man who had all the world offered and who was probably used to taking what he wanted, he entered her with a reverence that almost brought tears to her eyes.

The first touch of his tongue against hers nearly drove her to her knees. Passion exploded—a passion she'd never experienced before. Her throat was too tight for her to speak coherently, but a small sound of pleasure escaped. Perhaps he'd been waiting for that, or perhaps it was simply luck on her part. Either way, he dropped his hands to her waist and pulled her hard against him. Then he plunged his tongue fully into her mouth and claimed her.

Cynthia leaned against him because she couldn't stand on her own. She couldn't breathe or think or act. She could only feel the glory that was Jonathan as he continued to kiss her. She could only kiss him back and know that whatever else happened in her life, she would always have this night and the magic of his kiss. There had been other kisses before, other boys or men, but comparing their attentions to his was to compare a glass of water with the wonders of an ocean.

"Who *are* you?" he breathed against her mouth. "What are you doing to me?"

"I don't know," she said honestly and opened her eyes to look at him.

She had a brief impression of barely controlled passion and a desire that made her tremble with both anticipation and fear. Then there was a loud crack and all the lights went out in the ballroom.

## Chapter 2

"Well, hell," Jonathan said, staring into complete blackness. The interruption had been ill timed, to say the least. Or maybe it had been for the best. After all what had started out as a simple friendly kiss had turned into something much more. Something passionate and intriguing. Given the chance, he would have been very pleased to do a whole lot more than just kiss the mysterious Cynthia. That despite the obvious innocence in her eyes and the blushes staining her cheeks.

"What do you think happened?" Cynthia asked, her voice almost a whisper. "The hotel is new. Maybe this big charity event was more than the circuits could handle."

"Possibly," he said, but he was doubtful. Not that he could come up with a better explanation. Most of his blood was well south of his brain—a condition brought on by Cynthia's breasts still pressed firmly against his chest—which meant he wasn't thinking straight.

"It could be another blackout," she offered, referring to the thirty-six-hour blackout that had kept the city in chaos three years ago.

But Jonathan didn't respond. Something, more feeling than proof, whispered in the back of his mind. Suddenly he knew with a certainty that he couldn't explain that this blackout was very different from the one Cynthia mentioned. This one had a more sinister cause and he would bet most of his considerable fortune that David was somehow involved.

He stared at the woman he held, but he couldn't make out any of her features in the darkness. "Stay here," he told her. "Guests are going to panic and if you leave the alcove you could be trampled."

"But you're going to brave the madding crowd?" she asked.

"I don't have a choice," he said by way of explanation. He wasn't about to go into detail on the subject of his brother.

"Okay. I'll stay here."

He squeezed her upper arms, then pushed through the wall of plants that hid the entrance of the alcove. Already he could hear the increased volume of conversation as worried guests wondered what to do. Across the ballroom, a woman shrieked.

Using instinct and a faint light in the distance, Jonathan made his way along the perimeter of the ballroom. As he moved, he brushed against bodies and nearly tumbled over a tray perched precariously on a rickety stand.

A sense of urgency filled him, forcing him to walk faster and faster toward the flickering light. As he approached he realized he'd been drawn to the back of the ballroom, not the entrance that led into the hotel foyer. The flickering was caused by a door banging in the stiff evening breeze. Jonathan reached to push it open when the sharp sound of gunfire stopped him dead in his tracks.

He waited, counting three shots. Behind him, several people in the crowd screamed. He sensed a general surge of movement away from the danger and had a brief hope that Cynthia had stayed in the alcove. She would be a hell of a lot safer there than trying to fight her way out of the dark ballroom. He waited several more seconds until he thought it might be clear, then he stepped out into the parking lot behind the hotel.

His first thought was that there were too many lights and he slipped into a shadow by the door. So the power outage was localized to the hotel, or maybe just the ballroom. There were probably a hundred cars parked out here. Trees lined the edge of the parking lot. He sensed more than saw several flickers of movement. A tightness in his gut gave him a bad feeling about the entire situation and he couldn't get rid of the impression that somehow David was involved. Was the blackout a distraction for whomever was going to kill Jonathan? He shook his head. David would want to be far away before anything happened to his half brother.

"So what am I doing out here?" he muttered to himself.

Good question. He didn't have any way to protect himself against whoever had the gun. Nor was he a police officer with any kind of training. He was rarely impulsive and this unplanned action could get him dead very quickly. Still he stayed where he was, trying to figure out what exactly had happened.

He didn't have to wait long. A car door banged closed at the far end of the parking lot and he heard the

rumble of an engine, followed by a squeal of tires as
the vehicle sped away. Closer to him, he heard a man
swearing loudly.

"If anyone can hear me, call 9-1-1," he yelled.
"There are two injured people here. I've got to go after
the shooter."

Jonathan moved toward the voice. Before he'd gone
more than twenty feet, a second car took off into the
night. But Jonathan didn't spare it a glance. Instead he
looked down and saw two people sprawled out on the
tarmac. Two tall, dark-haired people. A man and a
woman.

His gut tightened even more and before he got close
he knew what he would find. He shifted and light fell
across the bodies. He recognized them both. David and
Lisa. Lying still. Too still.

"You all right?" Detective Jack Stryker asked Jonathan a couple of hours later.

Jonathan looked at the detective and shrugged. "Under the circumstances? I've been better."

Stryker, a tall man in his mid-thirties, nodded sympathetically. "I know this isn't easy. It was one thing
when you found out David was embezzling from the
company, but threatening to kill you makes it a whole
different story."

Jonathan didn't respond. All he could think of to ask
was if Stryker had a brother and did they get along.
Which was crazy. Other people's families didn't matter
to him. He had a half brother who had just threatened
to kill him. Now that half brother was in a hospital
somewhere, or already dead. He had the brief thought
that he should insist that the detective take him over to

the hospital to stand vigil or something, but he was still too numb to feel any sense of urgency.

If David was still alive, what was he, Jonathan, supposed to say to him? "I forgive you?" Would David give a damn about that? Jonathan doubted it. Besides, he wasn't sure he was willing to forgive. Not the death threat nor the stealing. Certainly not the lifetime of squandering every opportunity.

Stryker's cell phone rang. The detective answered it. Jonathan waited, leaning back in his chair and rubbing a steady pain by his temples. At least the lights had come on about an hour before. The room the two of them occupied was small and windowless. Probably a business conference center at the hotel. There was a long table in the center of the room and a dozen chairs pulled up around it. The serviceable carpet was a medium shade of gray. Still new enough not to be stained or flat in patches.

Carpet, Jonathan thought to himself. I'm thinking about carpet. What the hell is wrong with me?

But he knew the answer to that. If he didn't think about carpet, he might think about his brother again. About what David had done or wanted to do. About a threat of murder that was probably a whole lot more than a threat. About how things had gotten so screwed up and how he didn't have a clue as to how to fix them.

"What time?" Stryker asked.

An edge in the detective's tone alerted Jonathan. He turned in his seat until he faced the blond man leaning against the edge of the table. Stryker's face tightened.

"I see. All right." He paused. "Yeah. I'll tell him."

He continued talking, but Jonathan stopped listening. He knew the subject of the conversation and he knew what Jack Stryker planned to say. David and Lisa were both dead.

The news wasn't a surprise, he thought grimly as he waited for the realization to slam into him. He'd heard the gunshots. He'd seen their too-still bodies lying on the ground and the pools of blood around them. He'd known the truth the second he'd stumbled across their bodies. So he wasn't surprised to have the information confirmed.

Stryker shoved the phone into his jacket pocket. "Jonathan, I'm sorry."

Jonathan held up a hand. "I know. They're dead."

Stryker nodded. "They were pronounced dead on arrival at Vanderbilt Memorial. There will be an autopsy. It might delay things for a day or two."

It took Jonathan a second to figure out that the detective was talking about a funeral. Nothing could be scheduled until the bodies were released.

He swore under his breath. "What happened?" he asked and realized a second too late the detective would think he meant his brother's death, when Jonathan was really talking about a lifetime of a relationship gone wrong.

"There was luggage in the car," Stryker told him. "Eight good-size suitcases, passports and tickets to Rio. Several witnesses reported seeing them with a smaller, soft-sided black bag, but we haven't found that yet. Maybe it got kicked under one of the cars. We have officers searching the area."

Jonathan decided it was easier to talk about the murder than to explain what he'd really been asking. "Do you think it held the money?"

"Maybe." Stryker settled on a corner of the table. "David said he and Lisa were going to be far away when I was killed. Being out of the country would make their alibi even better. But who killed them?''

''We're going to have to find that out. We're looking for the two cars you saw leaving right after the shooting. Obviously David and Lisa weren't working alone. There had to be at least one other person involved, possibly more than that.''

One other person. The murderer. ''So if my brother was telling the truth about going away, then he was probably also telling the truth about having me killed.''

Stryker's steady blue gaze locked with his. ''That's my read on it.''

Jonathan couldn't escape his feeling of disbelief. This wasn't happening. ''Where would David find someone willing to kill me. Neither of us travel in the 'gun for hire' circle.''

''Unfortunately it's not as difficult as you might think. A couple of discreet questions in the right bar and you have a contact. One contact leads to another. If someone was motivated, he could set up a hit in a couple of days.''

''David was motivated,'' Jonathan said, trying to figure out why he wasn't more worried. Right now all he felt was numb. How had he and his brother turned out so differently? When had David started to hate him enough to want him dead?

''To make it more complicated,'' Stryker was saying, ''there's no way of knowing if David's death ended the threat or not. You'll need to hire a bodyguard. The department can help, but a full-time professional is your best bet. I know some good people. They're not local, but they can be here by morning.''

''Good idea,'' Jonathan said, even though he didn't believe the words as he spoke them. Protection? From a hired gun? That happened in the movies, not in real life.

"Let me get their phone numbers," Stryker said as he headed for the door leading in to the hallway. "I want to check a few things, too, so I may be a minute." He paused and looked at Jonathan. "There will be a uniformed officer outside the door. He's there to keep you safe so don't go wandering off without him."

"Not a problem," Jonathan said.

He didn't feel like wandering anywhere at the moment. He was too busy trying to absorb all that had happened. David and Lisa both dead. Was it possible?

Stryker stepped out into the hallway. Jonathan heard him talking with someone, then saw a flash of aqua. His brain quickly shifted gears, providing a name and a face to go with aqua tulle and silk. Cynthia? What was she doing here?

Before he knew what he was doing, he was on his feet and pulling open the door. Stryker and the uniformed officer had Cynthia pressed up against the hall wall. Jonathan couldn't see her face, but he realized she was shaking. She carried a cup of coffee in one hand and the cup rattled against the saucer.

"Stryker, she's with me," he said quickly.

The detective glanced at him. "Are you sure? She was lurking in the hallway."

"I didn't mean to do anything wrong," Cynthia said, her voice trembling as much as her hands. She stared at Stryker. "I was worried about Mr. Steele. He went outside when the lights went out and then there were gunshots. I heard the police had brought him to a conference room and I just wanted to make sure that he was okay." She turned her attention to Jonathan. "That's all. I'm sorry if I made trouble or anything."

Her dress looked out of place away from the ball and she still wore a ridiculous rhinestone tiara. Despite the fake jewelry, the smudges of mascara under her impossibly large hazel-green eyes and the patches on her long gloves, she was both lovely and sincere.

"Does she look dangerous?" he asked the detective.

"Ask me if that matters," Stryker told him. "But if you know her, then it's fine." He motioned for Cynthia to join Jonathan in the small conference room, then he glanced at the uniformed officer. "No one else gets in there. Just me. You got a radio?"

"Yup." The man touched the radio, then his gun. "I'll keep him safe."

"You do that."

As Stryker turned to leave, Jonathan ushered Cynthia into the small room.

"Why are you still here?" he asked when he'd shut the door and settled her into a chair. "I've been with the detective for a couple of hours. You must be tired."

Cynthia set the cup of coffee on the table. "I was worried," she said, repeating what she'd told Stryker. "I saw the ambulance, but when I asked I was told you were fine. Even so, I wanted to see for myself. I'd heard a lot of people were injured in the panic after the lights went out. Thanks for telling me to stay in the alcove. You saved me."

He waited for her to go on—to state her angle or what she wanted, but she was silent after that. While he believed her concern, mostly because it seemed genuine and he wanted to, he didn't doubt she had a purpose for being here. "Do you need cab fare back to your place?"

She frowned in confusion. "Of course not. I have my own car and if I didn't, I wouldn't make you responsible for getting me back home." She stared directly at him. "I don't want anything from you. I meant what I said. I stayed to make sure you were all right."

She meant it, he thought in amazement. Cynthia didn't want money or attention or any of the other dozen things women expected when they were with him. She had actually been worried. With no thought of personal gain. Was it possible?

"Who *are* you?" he asked.

She smiled. "Obviously not Cinderella. It's after midnight and I'm still here." She waved a foot. "Shoes and all." She pushed the cup of coffee toward him. "Here. This is for you. One of the waiters brought it for you and I said I'd bring it in." She gave a tiny shrug. "It was my excuse to get closer to the room with the hope of seeing for myself that you were fine."

He settled in the chair across from hers but didn't touch the coffee. "I appreciate your concern."

She leaned forward, resting her elbows on the table. "I have to say, this is my first society function and it didn't go exactly as I'd pictured it."

"We don't usually have murders here in Grand Springs. At least not at functions like this."

Cynthia shivered. "So those poor people are dead? How awful. Do the police know what happened?"

He pushed the coffee back toward her. "Here. Drink this. You need it more than I do."

She hesitated, then thanked him and picked up the cup.

"The police are still working on the details," Jonathan said.

"Do they know who the people are?" she asked before taking a drink of the coffee.

"Yes. My half brother and his wife."

Cynthia made a soft sound, then set the cup on the table. She stretched her arm across the table and placed her hand over his. "Oh, Jonathan. I'm so terribly sorry. You must be in shock."

She blinked and he would have sworn there were actual tears in her eyes. As if she was wounded on his behalf. Did women really cry for reasons other than manipulation?

She squeezed his fingers, then released him. "I can't know what you're going through right now," she said. "No one can. I lost my stepfather three years ago. I still remember the incredible pain and sense of loss. His being gone left such an incredible hole in my life. One that will never be filled." She sipped the coffee again. "Frank, my stepfather, was more like an older brother than a father to me. We were so close and I loved him deeply. I comfort myself with the fact that I was able to tell him that at the end."

She gave a soft cry, then pressed her free hand to her mouth. "I'm sorry," she said quickly. "That was so thoughtless. I didn't mean to make you feel worse by pointing out the fact that you didn't get to tell your brother goodbye."

A single tear trickled down her cheek. She set the cup back on the saucer and brushed away the dampness.

Jonathan watched her with the interest of an alien visitor examining an unfamiliar species. He'd heard her words, knew their meaning, yet he couldn't relate to anything she'd said. Her grief for her stepfather was genuine, as was her compassion for him. Yet nothing she said made sense to him.

"You're not thoughtless," he told her. "My brother and I weren't close."

There was an understatement, he thought. David had

embezzled millions from him and had arranged to have him killed. Other than that they'd been what...like brothers? Not in this lifetime.

"How can you not be close?" she asked. "You grew up together, didn't you? All families are close." She paused as if considering her statement. "Okay, maybe not all. My mom had me when she was very young and when she turned eighteen, her family threw her out of the house. Even though she had a small child to raise. So I guess I can understand about you and your brother. It just seems so sad."

She would be more upset if she knew the truth, he thought.

She stood up and paced to the far end of the room. Once there, she turned to face him. "I don't mean to presume, but do you have any family to help you out?"

"Help me with what?"

She folded her arms over her chest. In her ball gown and tiara she should have looked foolish. Instead he found himself thinking that she was lovely and still looked too innocent for the likes of him.

She cleared her throat. "With the arrangements. I'm only asking because, well, you're the kind of person who is known in the community. There have been a lot of articles about you in the newspaper and none of them has mentioned family, so I thought if you were alone, if there wasn't someone to help, I would be happy to do that. Not that I'm trying to butt in or anything."

She spoke quickly, as if she felt she had to get all the words out before he stopped her. Her posture was faintly defensive, yet he was the one wondering what *she* wanted from *him*.

When he didn't speak, she drew in a breath. "There's the funeral, then your brother's things to go through. I don't mean legal papers or a will, but rooms and closets. I remember how hard that was for my mom. I took care of it for her."

"I hadn't thought of any of it," he said truthfully. A funeral. He would have to see about that. It would be expected. And perhaps for Lisa as well. As far as he could remember, she didn't have any family, either. "Hell."

She was at his side in a minute. She lightly touched his arm and gazed at him with sympathetic concern. "I'm so sorry."

Her words and her barely there physical contact were all meant to comfort. Oddly enough, he *felt* comforted. He almost reached out to pull her close when the door opened and Stryker walked into the room.

"I've got some news," the detective said, then stopped when he saw Cynthia.

"I'll go wait outside," she said instantly.

Jonathan surprised them all, including himself, when he shook his head. "You can stay."

Stryker raised his eyebrows but didn't otherwise comment. "All right. We've checked out the tickets to Rio. They're one-way only, paid in cash. No hotel reservations, but an address of a private villa. We're looking into that. Probably arranged through friends or a real estate agent who specializes in renting to those who wish to disappear. They left money in their joint checking account, but several large transfers have come through in the past month."

Jonathan frowned. "As if they were cashing out other accounts? Funneling funds into one central bank, then removing them?"

"Exactly. It's going to take us a few days to trace everything back to its source."

"What about—"

But a soft cry interrupted his question. While he and Stryker had been talking, Cynthia had moved to the side of the room. Now she leaned against the wall and clutched her stomach. All the color had faded from her face, leaving her skin faintly gray.

Jonathan hurried toward her. "What's wrong?"

"I don't know," she gasped. "It hurts. One minute I was feeling fine and the next—" She moaned and dropped to her knees.

"Call an ambulance," Jonathan instructed.

"Already on it."

He heard Stryker speaking into his cell phone. Cynthia huddled on the floor. When he tried to move close to her, she cried out again. A sense of helplessness filled him.

"What can I do?" he asked.

She raised her head to look at him. Pain glazed her eyes. She opened her mouth, either to say something or cry out again. Instead she sucked in a breath and fainted. Jonathan caught her as she fell. He pulled her close and stroked her damp face.

First his brother and Lisa, now Cynthia.

"The ambulance is on its way," Stryker said, crouching next to them. "How's she doing?"

"She collapsed. I don't know what's wrong with her, but I have a bad feeling it has something to do with everything going on here tonight."

He looked at the detective and knew the other man shared his sense of dread about the situation. The hell of it was there was nothing either of them could do except stay with Cynthia and wait for help to arrive.

## Chapter 3

"There has to be something you can do," Jonathan insisted, even as he knew that losing his temper wasn't going to make the situation any better.

"Right now our goal is to keep her stable while we wait for test results," Dr. Noah Howell said calmly. "Once we know what is causing the problem, we can start treatment. Until we're sure, we're at risk of doing the wrong thing by acting without knowing what's really wrong with her."

Jonathan had never felt more frustrated in his life. He'd spent the last several hours dealing with situations he couldn't control and now he was faced with one more. He knew if he could just *do* something, he would feel better. But he wasn't a cop and he wasn't a doctor. He hated feeling like this.

"Is she still unconscious?" he asked.

Dr. Howell nodded. "However, under the circumstances, that's not surprising."

It might not be surprising, Jonathan thought grimly, but it also wasn't very good. Since fainting at the hotel, Cynthia had not regained consciousness. He'd accompanied her to the hospital where Noah Howell had examined her. For reasons that weren't clear to anyone, her entire body was in the process of shutting down. If they didn't figure out what was wrong soon, she was going to die.

A sense of powerlessness filled him. What was the point of being one of the richest men in Colorado if he couldn't save Cynthia's life?

"I have to get back to her," Dr. Howell said. "I'll let you know if there's any change."

"What about when you get the test results?"

Noah's blue eyes regarded him steadily. "I know you're concerned about Ms. Morgan. We're doing everything we can to save her. I'll be sure to keep you informed of her condition and any test results. If you or the detective come up with anything from your end, let me know."

Jonathan sank into one of the green plastic chairs that filled the small waiting room and swore under his breath.

"Hell of a day," Stryker said sympathetically. "First your brother and his wife, and now this."

Jonathan nodded, then leaned his head against the white wall. "I hate hospitals," he said, taking in the nondescript linoleum flooring and the television bolted to the wall on the opposite side of the room. It was on but mercifully silent.

Noises filtered in from beyond the confines of the waiting area. The squeak of soft-soled shoes, the clank of a piece of equipment being moved. He could smell the lingering scent of antiseptic and the previous eve-

ning's dinner. It was nearly two in the morning and the
waiting room was deserted. There was still chaos downstairs in the emergency room—people being treated in
the aftermath of the hotel blackout and the subsequent
panic. But up here was relative peace. At least he didn't
have to worry about making small talk with anyone.
Except Stryker.

He glanced at the detective. "I don't think you're
waiting with me because you're concerned about Cynthia Morgan."

"I wouldn't mind knowing she's okay," Stryker told
him. "But I'm here because I need to ask you some
questions."

Jonathan rubbed the bridge of his nose, as if he could
erase the weariness that filled him. "It feels like it
should be some time next week," he said. "Instead of
just early Sunday." He drew in a deep breath and figured there was no point in ignoring the obvious. "You
want to know if there was some reason David could
have wanted to get to me through her. Did he hurt Cynthia because it would bother me."

"The thought has crossed my mind," the detective
admitted. "Your brother obviously wanted to screw you
any way he could. The doctor said they didn't know
what was wrong with her. They've ruled out appendi-
citis. Once the tests come back we'll have a clearer
picture, but until then I can't rule out the suspicion that
David was involved."

Jonathan looked at Stryker and shook his head. "Not
possible. I just met her tonight." He told the other man
about literally running into Cynthia at the ball. How
he'd planned to leave, then had surprised himself asking
her to dance.

Without wanting to, he found himself caught up in

the past, in the pleasure of her in his arms. How she'd looked and felt as they moved together. The sweet scent of her skin and the way she'd tasted when he'd kissed her.

"David couldn't have known about her because I didn't," he concluded.

Stryker loosened his shirt collar, then jerked his head at the purse lying next to him. "There's nothing in there to give us a clue, either. I've notified her family. They're on their way here. Maybe they'll know something. Although her mother said Cynthia is perfectly healthy. Never had a medical condition."

Jonathan didn't want her to die. Not that he wished anyone dead, but his desire for Cynthia to live was strong and growing. He willed strength to her, as if he could send the power through the corridors of the hospital and help her hang on until the doctors got it all figured out.

The detective pulled out his notebook. "Start from the beginning and tell me again what happened."

"I was speaking with my brother," Jonathan began patiently, prepared to go through the sequence of events as many times as it took. "We'd just finished and I knew that if I was going to die that night I didn't want it to be at that ridiculous party. So I started to leave. When I turned I ran into—"

"Mr. Steele?"

He looked up and saw a young nurse standing in the doorway of the waiting area. Jonathan was on his feet in a heartbeat. "What? Do you have news?"

She nodded. "Dr. Howell asked me to tell you that the preliminary toxicology reports suggest that Ms. Morgan was poisoned. He wanted to let you and the detective know."

The news shouldn't have stunned Jonathan. After all he and Stryker had been talking about David being involved. But David couldn't have known about Cynthia. "Poisoned?" he repeated blankly.

She nodded. "He said that it would be helpful if you could figure out how and then find the poison." She gave him a quick, impersonal smile and turned to leave.

"Wait," he called. "How is she?"

"I don't know. The same, I think." And then she was gone.

Jonathan sank back into his chair. He looked at Stryker. "Poison? Does that make sense to you?"

"Depends on how it was delivered. Did she eat anything at the party?"

"I don't know," Jonathan admitted. He frowned in concentration. "When I first met her she was carrying a glass of wine. White, I think. She spilled it, so I doubt she drank much. If she ate before or after I was with her, then I wouldn't have seen what it was. While we were together, she didn't eat or drink anything."

Stryker tapped a pen on his notebook. His tweed jacket looked rumpled and blond stubble darkened his jawline. He rubbed his tired eyes. "We haven't had any complaints about other people getting sick. So it probably wasn't in the food. And if she ingested the poison before the party, we don't have a snowball's chance in hell of figuring out what it was."

Jonathan listened as the other man spoke, but a part of his brain focused on something else. A whisper of a memory that he couldn't make focus. Something just out of reach that seemed important and yet—

"The coffee," he announced, cutting Stryker off in midsentence. "She brought me coffee."

"What?"

He turned toward the detective. "At the hotel. Remember? You went to check on something and she was waiting in the hall. She wanted to see how I was. She was holding a cup of coffee and told me that a waiter had brought it for me. But I hadn't ordered any." He frowned, trying to remember the exact sequence of how things had occurred. "I didn't want any because I hadn't ordered coffee. Then Cynthia ended up drinking it instead."

Stryker was on his cell phone in an instant. He spoke to a police officer still at the scene.

"We'll see if we can get hold of that cup," he said when he was finished.

"Is that how David planned to kill me?" Jonathan asked. "Poison?"

Stryker shook his head. "Your brother wouldn't have been that specific. I'm guessing the killer saw an opportunity and took it. We'll interview the staff. Someone had to have seen a new guy working tonight. We'll find him and get him to tell us what kind of poison he used."

He sounded confident, but Jonathan wasn't so sure. Besides, even if they found the killer, would it be in time to save Cynthia?

"I need to get back to the hotel," Stryker said as he came to his feet. "You've got my number. Call me when you know more about Ms. Morgan's condition."

Jonathan hated the thought of being left behind. "There has to be something I can do to help." He couldn't just sit around and wait. He always acted in a crisis. It was one of his strong suits.

"We'll handle it, Jonathan," Stryker said. "I promise I'll be in touch."

And then he was gone, walking out of the waiting

area and down the corridor. Jonathan watched him go. The tall man passed by a young mother with three children. The harried woman stopped at the nurses' station across from the waiting area.

She was petite, maybe five-one or -two, with short blond hair. Something about her was vaguely familiar, yet Jonathan was sure he'd never met her before. He glanced briefly at the gangly preteen girl standing on one side of the woman, then at the twin boys clinging to her other arm. Then he shrugged and settled back in his seat. He didn't like waiting around, but it looked like he didn't have a choice.

"Mr. Steele?"

He looked up and saw the woman and her children had entered the waiting room. He rose to his feet, not sure how she knew him. "I'm Jonathan Steele."

The woman trembled slightly. Tears filled her blue eyes and her face was pale. "I, ah, they said at the desk that you brought her in. Cynthia. That you were with her." The woman paused and swallowed. Her visible effort to maintain control made him uncomfortable. "They didn't tell me anything when they called. Just that she'd collapsed and was being brought here. They wanted to know about existing medical conditions, but I told them she'd always been fine. A healthy girl, and, oh Lord, I can't lose her, too."

"It's okay, Momma," the preteen girl said and wrapped her arms around her mother's waist. "She'll be fine. You'll see." But she was crying as she spoke and the two boys clung tighter as tears spilled down the woman's face.

Jonathan resisted the need to bolt. He wasn't comfortable in the face of this much emotion or suffering.

"Look, maybe I should call a nurse or something," he said awkwardly, already backing from the room.

The woman was shaking her head. "No, I'm fine." She wiped her face with her free hand and offered him a poor imitation of a smile. More tears filled her eyes. "I'm sorry. I just can't seem to find the strength to deal with this. I suppose it's because I lost my husband three years ago and being in the hospital is bringing it all back."

Jonathan stared at her. Cynthia had mentioned something about her stepfather dying three years ago. Which meant this woman was her mother. But Mrs. Morgan didn't look much over thirty-five and Cynthia had to be in her mid-twenties.

"You're her mother?" he asked.

The woman nodded. "I was still a teenager when I had her. These three are my children with Frank."

A shudder rippled through her. Both the boys had tears on their faces and the preteen had given up pretending not to be crying. Jonathan felt as if he'd just boarded a leaking ship. In a matter of minutes they would all be going under.

"As someone must have told you, I'm Jonathan Steele," he said, touching the woman's arm and urging her and her children over to the plastic chairs.

" You can call me Betsy," she said, sinking onto the seat. "This is Jenny and the boys are Brad and Brett."

Jonathan gave the kids a reassuring smile. He crouched down in front of the distraught family. "I've spoken with the doctor in charge. His name is Noah Howell and he's about as good as they come. As of a few minutes ago, they know what's wrong with Cynthia and they're doing everything they can to make her better.''

Betsy stared at him. He saw now that her daughter had her mother's mouth and her eyes were the same shape, if a different color. Cynthia topped Betsy by about five inches, but they both had slender yet curvy figures.

"What happened?" Betsy asked. "Do they know why she's sick?"

He hesitated. There was no point in trying to hide the truth. They would find it out eventually. "They think she was poisoned. It was an accident," he added hastily. "But now they can start working on the best way to get the poison out of her system."

A voice came over the loudspeaker, requesting a doctor on a different floor. Betsy closed her eyes and shook her head. "I can't go through this again," she murmured, more to herself than to him. "I just can't."

"Mommy?"

One of the boys spoke. Betsy didn't respond verbally. Instead she put her arm around him and held him close. The little family seemed to fold in on itself, as if each member gathered strength from the others. Jonathan felt like an intruder.

He stood and cleared his throat. "Now that you're here to see about your daughter, I'll just be going," he said.

Betsy's eyes popped open. She stared at him. "You're leaving us?"

Both boys stared at him beseechingly. "Aren't you Cynthia's friend?" one of them asked.

Jonathan shifted uncomfortably. "Yes, well, we are friends and of course I'm concerned. It's just…" His voice trailed off.

The preteen girl didn't stay anything. She simply stared at him, tears running down her cheeks.

Betsy recovered first. "Of course, Mr. Steele. I'm sure you're a very busy man. It was kind of you to stay this long. Thank you for your concern. We'll be fine."

He wanted to swear at them all. They looked anything but fine. It was the middle of the night and they were all scared out of their minds. The kids had already lost their father and now they had to worry about their older sister. The mother looked as if she was going to lose it at any second.

He told himself this wasn't his problem. On the heels of that thought came the realization that Cynthia could have swallowed poison meant for him and there was no way these people were going to make it without some kind of help. For now, he didn't have a choice.

He shoved his hands into his tuxedo pants pockets. "I'm going to get some coffee," he said. "Why don't I bring you back a cup?" Then he glanced at the two boys. "You two want a soda or something? Why don't you come along and help me carry everything."

Betsy Morgan gave him a genuine smile. "Thank you, Mr. Steele. Those newspaper articles always say you're a wonderful, caring man and now I know they must be true."

"Call me Jonathan," he said curtly, wondering how he could explain that he was anything but wonderful and caring. In fact he was something of a bastard. But this was neither the time nor the place. Besides, if he stuck around long enough, she would figure it out for herself.

"But what does it *mean?*" Betsy asked the next morning.

There weren't any windows in the waiting room so it was impossible to tell what it was like outside. Jonathan glanced at his watch. Eleven-fifty. Sunday. Barely twelve hours since the ball last night, but he felt as if he'd already lived a lifetime since then.

"Stabilized means just that," Jonathan said, trying to keep Cynthia's mother calm. If she stayed in control, the kids were fine. When she started to lose it, he had four sobbing messes on his hands.

"Last night she was deteriorating," he reminded her. "So stabilized is a step up. Next, she'll start improving." At least he hoped so. He had enough skin in the game now that he wanted to make sure that Cynthia made a full recovery.

Betsy looked at him, then folded her arms over her chest and sighed. "You're being very patient and kind and I really appreciate that. I'm trying to believe what you're saying, but it's so hard. I want her to wake up."

"I know. Me, too. At least they've been letting us in to see her."

Just after breakfast Noah Howell had arrived in the waiting area with the news that they could visit Cynthia for a few minutes every hour.

Betsy tucked a strand of short blond hair behind her ears. She looked weary, with dark circles under her eyes. Last night she'd obviously dressed in haste. She wore a sweatshirt over jeans, and athletic shoes with no socks. Jonathan felt out of place in his tux. He knew that he would have to go home to shower and change at some point, but he wasn't ready to leave just yet.

The three kids were seated close to the television, watching a cartoon show. They all looked dazed from what was happening. Dazed and young and impossibly vulnerable. Their concern about their sister touched him, as did Betsy's love for her child.

"I can't survive if something happens to her," Betsy said in a low voice. "I won't make it."

Jonathan leaned close. "First, she's doing better and the doctors think she's going to be fine." Fine was a stretch, he admitted to himself. The fact that she was still unconscious wasn't good, but he wasn't about to remind Betsy of that. "Second, you'll make it because you have three children depending on you and you're not the kind of person who walks away from her responsibilities."

Tears filled her eyes. "I don't know if I can be that strong."

"I know you'll do what you have to."

She sniffed and looked at her three children. "I guess you're right. It just feels so impossible."

Her pain slipped through his defenses and made his insides ache. She loved her children with a fierceness that startled him. He hadn't known it was supposed to be like that between a mother and her offspring. His mother had walked out of his life when he was only five, leaving behind an angry husband and a confused and sobbing little boy. His stepmother had been kind, but ineffectual against his father's tirades. Growing up, he hadn't had much in the way of emotional security and comfort.

Watching Betsy with her children made him wonder how life would have been different if his mother had stayed, or if his father had forgiven him for being the son of the woman who had left him.

Jonathan straightened in his chair and forced himself to push away the maudlin thoughts. It was all the inactivity, he told himself. It gave a man too much time to think.

Movement by the waiting room door caused Jonathan to look up. He saw Jack Stryker standing in the hallway, motioning to him. Jonathan excused himself and stepped out to speak with the detective.

"You look like hell," Stryker said by way of a greeting. "Have you had any sleep at all?"

Jonathan dismissed the question. "I'll get home later today for a quick shower. That's all I need right now. What did you find out?"

Stryker grinned. "I have good news for you, my man. We have recently taken into custody one Harold P. Millingsgate, better known as Harry the Hood. He has as many arrests as he has tattoos, which is saying something. He's a career criminal, starting out with small stuff in high school and graduating to some impressive felonies. In the past couple of years, he's moved into killing for hire. He's wanted for murder in several states, including Texas and he's willing to talk to avoid extradition to a place where they are more eager to enforce the death penalty."

"He's the one who poisoned the coffee?"

"He sure is. He's already handed over the substance—some chemical used for industrial pest management—which I took to Dr. Howell. After looking at a series of photos, Harry identified your brother as the man who hired him to kill you. He was supposed to wait until later this week, but he wanted to head back to New York before the first of the winter storms, so he went to work a little early."

Jonathan didn't know what to say. While he was grateful that the doctors could now figure out how to make Cynthia better, he couldn't absorb the fact that

David had actually hired someone to kill him. Hearing it from his brother was one thing, but having a detective fill him in on the details was another.

He stood in the hallway waiting to feel something—anger, rage, frustration. But there was only cold emptiness. He'd always known that his brother had resented his presence. David had longed to be the only Steele son. But murder was a hell of a way to realize his dream.

"I guess he figured embezzling wasn't enough," he said with a lightness he didn't feel. "I appreciate all your hard work on this, Jack."

"It wasn't just me," the detective said. "Once we knew the poison came from the coffee, we had a place to start. Tracking down Harry after that was just a matter of following leads." He hesitated. "There's more. The good news for you is David hired Harry directly, so you don't have to worry about an assassin lurking in your future."

"What's the bad news?"

"David and Lisa were involved with some pretty dangerous people. Embezzling from Steele Enterprises was the least of it. I'm not at liberty to go into details, but the FBI is involved. In fact, they're going to want to talk to you in the next day or so."

"I'll talk to them whenever they want," Jonathan said, wondering what David had been up to. Obviously trying to destroy Steele Enterprises hadn't been enough. If he'd been willing to kill his own half brother, then he would be capable of a lot of other criminal activities.

"Are those dangerous people the reason David and his wife were killed?" he asked.

"We can't know for sure," Stryker told him, "but it

makes sense. I have a feeling that this mess isn't going to be cleaned up for a while.''

Jonathan thanked the man for his information, then returned to the waiting area. Betsy Morgan gazed at him with hopeful eyes.

''That was the police,'' he said. ''They've located the poison and now the doctors will have a clear idea about what to do for an antidote.''

''Thank you for telling me.'' She looked at him as if seeing him for the first time. ''You must be exhausted,'' she said. ''You don't have to stay here with us.''

He glanced from her to her three kids, huddled together, united by fear of losing their older sister. He might not be much, but from what he could tell, he was all they had.

''I'm not going anywhere,'' he told Betsy. ''Not until Cynthia is out of danger.

They all gathered around Cynthia's bed and waited. Even Detective Stryker lingered in the hallway. It was Monday afternoon. Cynthia had been unconscious for thirty-six hours, although in the past few hours she'd showed signs of coming to.

Jonathan stayed near the back of the room. He felt like an interloper at this very private family event. But every time he tried to leave, Betsy dragged him back.

''Don't even think about it,'' she said when he once again inched toward the door. ''You stuck with us through the last couple of days. The least we can do is let you be here when she wakes up.''

''Mommy, look!''

One of the twins cried out as Cynthia tossed her head and muttered under her breath.

Betsy was at her side in an instant. She took her

daughter's hand. "Come on, honey. Wake up. You have us all worried and we just want to make sure that you're feeling better. Then you can sleep some more. Come on, Cynthia. Wake up."

Jenny and the two boys stood pressed against one side of the bed while Betsy stood guard on the other. Jonathan leaned against the wall by the door and Stryker made calls on his cell phone from the hallway.

"Mom?"

He looked up in time to see Cynthia's eyelids flutter then open. Betsy beamed at her oldest, tears pouring down her cheeks.

"Why are you crying?" Cynthia asked, then turned to her right and saw Jenny and the boys. "Hey, what are you three doing here?" She blinked. "What am *I* doing here?"

"You've been sick," her mother said as she stroked her daughter's face. "But you're going to be fine and that's what matters."

Cynthia shifted slightly on the bed. "Sick? I guess I don't feel great, but it's not so bad. My stomach hurts, though. I remember…" Her voice trailed off. "I was at the party and talking to Jonathan Steele. His brother died. I wanted to make sure he was all right before I came home and…"

Her gaze moved around the room and settled on him. Her eyes widened. "Is that really you?"

He pushed away from the wall and leaned against the foot of her bed. "Last time I checked."

She gave him a weak smile. "What are you doing here?"

He jerked his head toward her family. "They've been really worried about you. I stayed because I thought maybe you really were trying to turn into a pumpkin."

His joke earned him a faint giggle.

He stepped back to let the others have more time with her. Now that she was awake and obviously feeling better he told himself it was time to leave. After all, she would want to be with her family, not some stranger she'd just met.

But it was more difficult to go than he'd thought. Something about the people clustered together around the bed called to him. He wanted to stand close and be a part of the moment. Which was ten kinds of crazy. He didn't need them. He didn't need anyone.

He glanced once more at the bed, taking in Jenny's big smile and Cynthia's delicate features. She was a little pale, but otherwise as pretty as she'd been the night he'd met her. A lot had happened since then.

"Everybody happy?" Stryker asked from the doorway.

"Looks that way." Jonathan stepped out into the hall to join the detective. "She's awake, which Dr. Howell said was the next step in her recovery. He'll check on her tonight. She might be released in the morning."

"Then we're down to the final details," Stryker told him. "You'll be hearing from protective services this evening. They'll want to get things going as quickly as possible."

Jonathan stared at the man. "What are you talking about?"

"The baby."

Jonathan heard the word, but it didn't make any sense. "What baby?"

"David and Lisa's son. Your nephew."

Stryker kept talking but Jonathan wasn't listening. A baby? He vaguely remembered David talking about Lisa being pregnant. He'd received a notification of the birth, along with a letter requesting a gift, but nothing else. He and David didn't spend much time together so he'd never actually seen his nephew.

"He's been in a temporary foster home for the last couple of days," the detective was saying, "but you're welcome to take custody anytime you'd like. As far as we can tell, you're his only living relative."

"There has to be someone else," Jonathan said forcefully. "I don't know anything about babies."

"Then you'd better learn, Jonathan, because you're his new legal guardian."

# Chapter 4

"They're very beautiful," Betsy said as she fussed over the huge bouquet that had been delivered to her daughter's room late that afternoon.

Cynthia leaned back in her hospital bed and gazed at the exotic flowers. "I agree." She grinned. "I don't even know what half of them are. I recognize starburst lilies and the roses, but what are those little waxy things? And all that purple puffy stuff?"

Betsy smiled at her. "Purple puffy stuff? Is that the official Latin name?"

"I guess it is for us."

Her mother moved to the side of her bed and patted her hand. "You seemed to have made an impression on Jonathan Steele."

"You think?" Cynthia asked, not meeting Betsy's gaze.

Thirty-six hours of unconsciousness had left her brain a little foggy. Certain events leading up to her passing out after drinking the poison weren't as clear as they could be. She remembered going to the ball and then meeting and dancing with Jonathan. She definitely remembered their kiss...perhaps in more detail than she should. But she didn't recall much more than stomach cramps, then waking up to find her entire family *and* Jonathan waiting in her hospital room.

"He stayed here the whole time you were unconscious," Betsy told her. She sighed and touched her daughter's cheek. "For a while they weren't sure you were going to make it and I didn't see how I could survive that. I was closer to falling apart than I would like to admit and your Mr. Steele was very supportive."

Cynthia felt a flare of heat on her cheeks. "He's not *my* anything."

"Then why the flowers?"

Cynthia returned her gaze to the beautiful display. "I guess he's just a nice man."

Her mother took her hand in hers and squeezed it slightly. "I'd have to agree with you on that."

Jenny, Brad and Brett returned from their trip to the hospital cafeteria for dessert. The boys gave their mother an elaborate description of the piece of pie they'd each had. Jenny was quieter, hanging back until Cynthia patted the edge of her mattress and urged her to sit down.

"I'm fine," she said quietly when the thirteen-year-old settled gingerly next to her. "I know it was scary, especially when no one knew what was wrong, but I'm okay now."

Big blue eyes stared at her face. Jenny flashed a quick smile, showing a mouthful of braces. "I know you're better, but for a while it was awful." She glanced at their mother. "If Mr. Steele hadn't been here, I think

Mom would have lost it. But he stuck around and made sure we all ate and stuff.'' Jenny flicked her long blond hair behind her shoulders.

Despite the age difference, she and Jenny were close. Cynthia had missed her terribly the year she'd been working in Chicago. Since Frank's death three years ago, Cynthia had been living in Grand Springs, giving her and Jenny a chance to renew their special relationship.

"I'll be home in the morning," she reminded her sister. "Life will be back to normal and you won't have an excuse to miss school."

"I'm glad you mentioned that," Betsy said as she ruffled Brett's short blond hair. "Visiting hours are about over and we need to get going. These three need a good night's sleep so they can be alert for classes tomorrow."

"Ah, Mom," Brad said. He puffed out his lower lip in an effort to show his mother how much the news distressed him, but she wasn't the least bit impressed.

"No 'ah Mom's' from you, young man." But her warm hug belied the stern tone of her voice. Both freckle-faced boys clung to her for a brief embrace before turning to their oldest sister.

"See you tomorrow, Cyn," Brad said. Brett leaned down and hugged her.

She squeezed the twin boys, then gave them each a smile. "I'll be home by the time you get back from school. Everything is going to be fine. You'll see."

It took a couple of minutes for the Morgan family to finish their goodbyes, but just before the end of visiting hours, Cynthia finally found herself alone. She sank back against her pillow and sighed with contentment. Despite the potential tragedy of what had happened to

her, everything had turned out well. She was nearly recovered from the poison and Dr. Howell had assured
her there would be no long-term effects. Her body felt
a little achy and her stomach would take a few days to
settle down, but they were minor complaints.

As she pulled the sheet and blanket up to her chin,
Cynthia turned her attention to the extravagant display
of flowers by the window. They had arrived that afternoon with a handwritten note from Jonathan Steele.
He'd ducked out that morning, shortly after she'd regained consciousness. Now, after everyone was gone,
she was willing to admit that she'd been hoping he
might stop by and see her before she left in the morning.
But that wasn't likely. Jonathan had a very busy life.
They were practically strangers. He'd already been so
kind to her family.

But all those reasons weren't enough to ease her faint
sense of disappointment. She'd wanted to see him
again. Mostly because she knew she would never have
another chance. They'd lived their entire lives in the
same town and had never run into each other before.
That wasn't about to change.

"Oh well," she said softly and closed her eyes. "Obviously I should have left my shoe at the ball or something."

She waited for sleep to claim her. She'd nearly drifted
off when she heard her door open quietly, followed by
the sound of footsteps on the linoleum.

She opened her eyes and blinked at her visitor. Jonathan Steele—tall, darkly handsome and carrying a
large stuffed bear—stood at the foot of her bed.

"I couldn't tell if you were really asleep or just pretending," he teased, then glanced over his shoulder toward the door. "I'm here after hours over the protest

of your nurse. She made me promise to stay no more than ten minutes. If I violate that, she's threatening bodily harm. Have you seen her? I think she could take me."

Cynthia found herself giggling even as her entire body tingled with delight. "Thank you for visiting me." Then she remembered her hospital gown, her lack of makeup and the fact that her hair must look like a visual "ode to a rat's nest."

"I'm a mess," she said, trying to smooth her bangs.

Jonathan pulled a chair up close to the bed and sat down. "Neither of us think you're anything but very lovely," he said, handing her the stuffed bear. "This is Alfie. He was put into one of those programs that release animals back into the wild, but he decided he would rather live with an attractive blond woman who works with children. I instantly thought of you. I hope you don't mind."

She wrapped her arms around the cuddly bear. "I don't mind at all. Thank you for him. And for the flowers. They're beautiful." She eyed the bouquet. "I'm not sure they'll fit in the car."

"I can rent you a truck if you need it."

"Gee, thanks." She pushed the control panel and raised her bed so that she was nearly in a sitting position. "And thank you for all your help with my family. Everyone says you were terrific. My mom says she was on the verge of falling apart and you helped her keep it all together."

Jonathan dismissed the comment with a flick of his hand. "No problem. All I did was go for coffee and keep the kids fed."

She shook her head. "You stayed. We're strangers to you and yet you stayed. That means a lot."

He leaned back in his plastic chair. During the time he'd been away he'd changed from his tux and had showered and shaved. Now a white shirt emphasized the width of his shoulders, while worn jeans outlined narrow hips and strong thighs. She wouldn't have thought of a rich powerful guy like him wearing jeans, but she had to admit he could easily have modeled them on billboards across the country. Men might not be impressed but most women would have slowed to take a second look.

But it wasn't just his body that got her attention. He wore his short, dark hair in layers. The hints of silver at the temple gave him a distinguished air. She found herself wondering if it was possible to get lost in his gray-blue eyes. She would have thought the color could be cold and distant, but on him it was warm and welcoming.

"I don't think my actions qualify me for sainthood," he said, "but thank you for the compliment."

"I'm impressed you weren't overwhelmed by my family." She smiled. "The boys, especially. Most people have trouble telling them apart and when they decide to get into trouble, there's no stopping them."

"They were on their best behavior. I think you had them scared."

"I guess you're right." She relaxed against her pillow. "When I was little, I was an only child. I was so happy when my mom had Jenny and then the boys. We're a close family."

His expression hardened. She couldn't read what he was thinking, but she knew that she'd reminded him of something unpleasant.

"I'm sorry," she said quickly. "That made you think of your brother. You're still in shock about his death."

"Among other things," he admitted. He hesitated, then leaned forward and rested his elbows on his knees. "David and Lisa have a son. Colton. He's three or four months old. Apparently I'm his only relative, and therefore his guardian."

Cynthia beamed at him. "How wonderful! Oh, Jonathan, this is great. You're going to have a piece of your brother in your life. As Colton grows up you'll be able to see parts of David in him. You must be so relieved to know you're going to have your nephew living with you."

"That's one way of looking at it."

He didn't sound very excited.

"Aren't you happy?"

"I'm getting used to the idea." He straightened. "The police have found the man who put the poison in the coffee." He paused, then looked at her. "It wasn't meant for you, Cynthia. I don't want you worrying that someone is out to get you."

She turned his words over in her mind. The pieces all clicked into place. "The poison was for you, wasn't it?"

He nodded.

"But they caught the man? You're safe now?"

"Looks that way. I'm sorry you drank the coffee. If I'd known—"

"But you didn't," she said, interrupting him. "It was just circumstances. I'm not thrilled I was sick, but I'm going to be fine. Dr. Howell is letting me go in the morning."

Jonathan nodded. "I heard. I've already spoken to your mother. I'll be handling your medical expenses."

"You don't have to do that. I have insurance."

"All the same, it's something I want to do."

She didn't know what to say to that. She didn't think he was offering charity. He was a rich man, so the money wouldn't mean as much to him as it would to her. She bit her lower lip. "Okay. I appreciate your kindness, but in return I want to do something for you."

A predatory gleam came into his eyes. A smile tugged at the corners of his mouth. "What did you have in mind?"

"Well, unless you've made other arrangements already, I might just have a solution to your problem."

"Which problem is that? I have several right now."

She smiled. "The problem of what to do about the baby. I'm guessing that no matter how thrilled you might be to have custody of him, you're not exactly equipped to take care of an infant."

His expression tightened. "That would be an understatement."

"I thought as much." She set the stuffed bear next to her and linked her hands together on her lap. "I happen to be the sole owner of a company called Mother's Helper. We provide temporary live-in nannies for just this sort of occasion. Actually we do a lot of work for parents with newborns or people who have a short-term day-care crisis. Your child care needs are going to be long-term, but I can help you until you can make permanent arrangements."

He frowned. "I thought you taught kindergarten."

"No," she said with a laugh. "You said I worked with children and I agreed. I actually work with babies the most." She paused and felt herself blushing. "I would be thrilled to help you out, Jonathan. I owe you. Not just because of what happened here in the hospital but because you're the reason I have my business at all. The seed money you provided for start-up companies here in Grand Springs made it possible for me to open Mother's Helper. I received a grant of capital as well as a lot of excellent business advice.''

He shifted uncomfortably on his chair. "Like I said, I'm not exactly saint material.''

"You are to me. One of my clients gave me a ticket to the charity ball. I came specifically with the hope that I would be able to meet you and thank you.''

"Look, Cynthia. You're a nice young woman and I'm sure you mean all this, but I'm not a nice guy. I could introduce you to a dozen people who would be happy to swear that I'm a real bastard.''

"They're wrong," she said simply and with great conviction. Jonathan had been nothing but kind from the moment she'd met him. "You're one of the good guys. An asset to the community and a real gentleman. Just like my stepfather.''

"How flattering," he said dryly. "This is where I remind you that you don't know me from a rock. Before you commission a statue to my greatness, you might want to get to know me a little better. You'll find that I tarnish on further acquaintance.''

"I don't believe you," she told him. His protestations simply convinced her that he was modest as well as good. "But I *am* still offering my company's services. Do you want me to provide you with a temporary live-in nanny?''

"Sure. Someone has to look after Colton. I have a business to run." He stood up, leaned over and kissed her cheek. "You can barely keep your eyes open, so I'm going to go before I get thrown out. I'll be by to talk with you in the morning. We can work out the arrangements.''

Her skin heated where he'd touched her and she

wished he'd kissed her on the mouth instead of the cheek. "You'll, ah, have to tell me what you're looking for in a nanny. I'm not sure who is available right now but I can find out and give you a list."

He looked at her and raised his eyebrows. "I don't bother with staff," he said. "I prefer to work with the people in charge."

Her mouth dropped open. "You want me to be the nanny? But that would mean living with you. In your house."

He smiled. "I know. Still think I'm a saint?"

Heat filled her. Heat from his nearness and her memories of the kiss they'd shared. Heat and a desire to say yes. Even if it was just for a few days, she wanted to see what it was like to spend time with someone like Jonathan Steele.

"I sometimes take jobs," she said slowly. "If we're really busy or it seems like I would be a good match for the client."

"I think we've already proven we're a good match," he said. "I'll see you tomorrow."

And with that he was gone. Cynthia was left alone with Alfie, the bear and her whirling thoughts. Jonathan was completely out of her league. She had no business trying to make herself fit into his world. If she tried, she was practically promising herself heartache. The man appealed to her in fifty different ways, yet she knew that he couldn't possibly share her feelings.

"A smart woman would simply walk away," she told the bear. And she'd always thought of herself as smart. Yet she knew she wasn't going to be this time. She could only hope that she wasn't going to regret her impulsiveness.

\* \* \*

What was he doing here? Jonathan asked himself the question late the next afternoon as he sat in the middle of the chaos that was the Morgan living room.

Brad and Brett, the ten-year-old twins were sprawled out on the carpet, arguing about a board game they were playing. Betsy was fussing, bringing drinks and snacks, while Cynthia stretched out on the sofa, a handmade afghan tucked around her legs. Jenny sat in the wing chair by the window.

He had no business being here, he thought, trying to avoid looking at both Cynthia and Jenny. He felt awkward and out of place. But he was trapped by a situation of his own making and he had no one to blame but himself. He'd been the one teasing Cynthia the previous night, playing a grown-up game with someone who was still very much an innocent. He'd allowed himself to consider the possibilities of having her under his roof, but he'd ignored the reality of who and what she was. He didn't have the right to seduce her and by suggesting she be the one to help him with his nephew, he'd invited her into his home. Now he was stuck with her and all the temptation she provided.

Even as he told himself to look away he found his gaze drawn back to her pretty face. She had wide hazel-green eyes, so different from the rest of the Morgan family. They all had blue eyes. Cynthia must take after her father in that way. She was also much taller than her mother—another legacy from her paternal side. But her features were similar to Betsy's. He also caught the likeness in the tilt of her head and her quick smile.

He told himself he had no business thinking of Cynthia that way. She was several years younger than himself. Her lack of worldliness widened the gap between them. If she was really going to work in his home, then he had to forget their kiss and the attraction he felt, and replace it with a cordial, worklike attitude.

A soft cooing sound caught his attention. Reluctantly he looked at Jenny and the wrapped bundle she held. Child services had delivered his nephew to him less than two hours before. At Cynthia's suggestion, the social worker had come to the Morgan house. Colton would spend the next couple of days here until Cynthia was well enough to begin her duties at Jonathan's house.

"Nervous?"

He turned at the sound of her voice and caught her watching him. "About?"

She smiled. "I've seen you trying to avoid looking at Colton. Small babies frequently make new fathers nervous, so I'm guessing he'll have the same effect on his uncle. After all, you told me that you hadn't spent much time around him."

Today was the first time he'd seen Colton, but he wasn't going to tell her that. Cynthia had her own particular views about families and their relationships. He didn't share her opinion, but he wasn't going to get into an argument, either. Not with Jenny and the twins as interested bystanders.

"I thought Colton would do better in the hands of a professional." He winked at Jenny. His gesture earned him a shy smile.

"He's a wonderful baby," the teenager said. "I've been going on jobs with Cynthia since she started her business and I've always loved being with the babies."

"Jenny's a natural," Cynthia told him.

Betsy bustled in with a plate of freshly baked cookies. Jonathan could see the steam still rising from them.

The boys scrambled to their feet at the sight and swarmed toward their mother.

"Company first," she said, stepping around them and approaching Jonathan. "I hope you like chocolate chip."

"Who doesn't?" he said lightly, taking two cookies.

She passed the plate around, then had to take it back from Brad and Brett when they each grabbed two handfuls. The boys were good-natured about replacing the extra cookies.

Jonathan took a bite of the still-warm cookie. While he appreciated the gesture, he felt out of place in the house. A part of him could appreciate the warmth of the well-worn furniture and the way the children obviously cared about each other. But appreciation was different from understanding. Here, in the small living room, with the open game box scattered and magazines stacked haphazardly on an end table, was the real heart of a home. His house might be several times larger, but that only gave it more room for the silence to echo. Not that he was interested in what these people had. He still believed that families were an invention of the devil.

Betsy wiped her hands on her jeans, then settled on the sofa by Cynthia's feet. She placed a hand on her daughter's knee. "Did Cynthia tell you that your contribution to start-up capital is the reason she was able to form Mother's Helper?"

Jonathan swallowed uncomfortably. "She mentioned it last night. It's not a big deal." Instead it was a nice tax write-off and a way to grease wheels in the community. Not that he could explain that to anyone in this room. He doubted any one of them had ever had a cynical thought in their collective lives.

"We think it's a very big deal," Betsy insisted.

"Jonathan's not interested in having a statue erected in his honor," Cynthia said, giving him a teasing smile. "He told me so last night."

He'd also told her that he was a bastard, but she hadn't bothered to listen. Or had she? Had she figured out that he was nothing like her? That he was dangerous? That the only thing that would prevent him from following up on their impressive kiss was a thin veneer of civility that said a man like him had no business preying on the innocents?

"Do you think he knows?" Jenny asked. She looked at the baby and blinked several times. "Colton. Do you think he knows his parents are gone?"

Jonathan was stunned to see tears in her eyes, as if the thought of the boy being on his own was painful to her.

"I know how I felt when Dad died," she whispered.

He didn't know what to say to that. If he wasn't careful they would start acting sympathetic, which he didn't want. He still didn't know how he felt about David being dead. His own brother had tried to steal millions of dollars and have him killed. In the process he'd gotten involved with some dangerous people and that had cost him his life.

Betsy stood up and reached for the plate of cookies. "All right. You boys come on with me. You, too, Jenny. We'll go into my bedroom and watch a movie while Cynthia and Mr. Steele talk about arrangements for Colton's care."

She ushered the boys out in front of her, then placed her free arm around Jenny's slender shoulders. The teenager held the baby as if he were her most precious possession. In her sweatshirt and jeans, she looked like the thirteen-year-old she was, yet her competence with the baby impressed him. He doubted he would ever do as well. Nor did he want to try.

"I'm sorry," Cynthia said when they were alone. "Jenny speaks without thinking."

"I'm fine," he answered honestly. "I hope she's not too upset."

"Sometimes Frank's death still gets to all of us. But Mom is good at distracting the kids." She hesitated. "I hope you don't mind that Jenny took Colton in with her. I thought she would feel better if she continued to hold him, but if you're concerned about her taking care of him—"

He held up his hand to stop her in midsentence. "I might not know anything about babies, but even I can see she knows what she's doing. In fact if it were in my power, I would be happy to leave him in her capable care until he was eighteen or so."

Cynthia grinned. "You'll get over being nervous. In a couple of weeks you won't be able to remember what it was like without him in your life."

He doubted that but didn't see the point in arguing.

She shifted on the sofa, pulling up the afghan and leaning back against the pillows one of the boys had brought her. "I expect Colton and I will be moving in this Friday. What do you want to do about baby furniture and supplies?"

He stared at her blankly. "Whatever you think is best."

"I figured as much." She smiled. "I can't see you having a great time hanging out at the baby store."

Nor could he. "Are you going to be up to all this?" he asked. "You're still recovering."

"I feel fine. I'm ready to get back to work."

He wasn't so sure. "Perhaps I should simply start

looking for a permanent nanny now and save you the trouble.''

Cynthia's gaze was steady. ''You can start looking whenever you'd like. In fact one of the services I provide is an interview screening process. I'm also happy to be at the interview with you. But finding someone to stay in your house, looking after your child on a long-term basis isn't all that easy. It usually takes time. I don't mind filling in.''

But this wasn't about her, he thought. Even now Cynthia was gazing at him with a look that spoke far more than she realized. She wasn't looking at him with hero worship—not exactly. It was more...female interest in an available man. And he would be willing to bet his third-quarter earnings that she didn't have a clue that he could tell what she was thinking.

She reached for her glass of water, but it was a couple of inches out of reach. When she started to move, he waved her back to the sofa.

''I'll get it,'' he said and crossed the room.

When he handed her the glass, he found himself sitting on the edge of the sofa instead of returning to his seat. Cynthia took a drink then put the glass down.

She wore jeans and a green sweatshirt that had faded from too many washings. There wasn't a speck of makeup on her face. Her shoulder-length blond hair was loose and soft around her face. She looked young and fragile and she'd nearly died because of him.

''I'm sorry about the poisoning,'' he said. ''I know that's a stupid thing to say, but I never wanted you to get hurt.''

She drew her knees to her chest. ''Don't be silly. It's not your fault. It was an accident.''

His hip pressed against hers. He could feel the heat

of her through the layers of her clothing and his own. He was close enough to inhale the floral fragrance of soap or shampoo or maybe just the essence of her.

She smiled. "Right up until the bad stuff started happening, I'd been having a really good time. I'd hoped I would meet you. I never thought we'd get to dance."

"Or that you would drink poison meant for me."

"Don't," she said with a shake of her head. "It doesn't matter."

"Yes, it does."

He found himself drawn to her, moving closer, when there wasn't that much room between them to begin with. She was trouble, he thought. She might look like the last living virgin, but she was more dangerous than any other woman he'd ever known.

"Did you like the dancing, too?" she asked, her voice breathless.

He was close enough to see that her eyes had dilated and that color was moving up her neck and down from her hairline. A blush. Who the hell still blushed?

"I liked the kissing better," he said honestly.

But before he could press his mouth to hers, there was a sound from a nearby room. He remembered where he was and who had the potential to walk in without warning. He drew back and rose to his feet.

"Coward," Cynthia said lightly.

"Let's just say I know about the importance of good timing. And this isn't it."

# Chapter 5

It was nearly eleven in the morning when Cynthia arrived at Jonathan's house on Friday. She pulled up in front of the huge three-story home and wondered if her aging but serviceable car was going to faint from shock at being in such impressive surroundings.

The brick façade was both grand and intimidating. A wide porch fronted by pillars stretched out twenty or thirty feet. "We come from different sides of the tracks," she told the baby gurgling contentedly from his car seat behind her. "You have lots of money in your family tree."

Colton was not impressed. His blue-eyed gaze settled on her face and he smiled. Then he blew a bubble out of his perfect rosebud mouth.

"You are too cute," she informed him as she collected her purse, then prepared to walk around to the passenger side of the car. Behind her a large truck rumbled into view. A truck filled with everything a baby could ever want.

While she hadn't seen Jonathan since the day she'd been released from the hospital, they'd been in touch by phone. Last night he'd called to tell her that he'd arranged for one of the larger baby stores in town to open an hour early this morning so that she could buy whatever Colton might need. He'd already faxed the store a floor plan and the dimensions of the baby's room to help visualize the space. Cynthia had been impressed with his efficiency.

The store owner had met her and Colton promptly at nine. Jonathan had left the same instruction with both women—there was no spending limit. Cynthia was to get whatever she thought was best.

Cynthia opened the rear passenger door and began unstrapping the baby. "Your uncle trusts my taste, doesn't he?" she cooed. "I think Uncle Jonathan was terrified I was going to make him come with me. Yes. Big, powerful Uncle Jonathan is afraid of baby things."

She lifted out Colton and held him close. The little boy smelled of baby powder and that indescribable scent that makes maternal types go weak at the knees with longing for a child of their own. She tickled him under the chin, making him laugh and wave his hands.

"I'm sure you had a good time," she told the baby as she carried him toward the front door. "I, however, couldn't help thinking that it would have been more fun for me if I'd had cart blanche in a ritzy department store." She was smiling as she reached for the doorbell.

But she never had a chance to press the button. The wide wood and beveled glass door flew open. A woman in her mid-fifties, wearing a black dress and white apron clapped her hands together.

"Oh, finally Mr. Jonathan brings me a baby. I've been begging him for years and always he ignores me. 'Lucinda,' he says. 'I'm not the baby type.' Maybe so, but I remind him that I am."

The woman, Jonathan's housekeeper Cynthia presumed, was about her height, with short dark hair and brown eyes the color of milk chocolate. Her wide smile made her eyes crinkle. She looked soft and plump—and Cynthia liked her on sight.

Lucinda reached for the child, then stopped and touched her forehead with her fingertips. "You must think I'm crazy, keeping you out here on the doorstep. You're Cynthia, right? Come in, come in. I'm Lucinda. I keep Mr. Jonathan's house. Not that there's very much to do. The man works all the time. He rarely eats at home. I send his clothes out to be cleaned. So where does that leave me? I watch my soaps in the afternoon. I tell him not to pay me so much money, what with me watching television, but does he listen?"

Cynthia took in the flow of conversation. She realized she wasn't actually expected to comment on any of it, which made her feel better. She wasn't sure she would know where to start.

"Yes, I'm Cynthia Morgan," she managed to inject. "This is Colton, Jonathan's nephew. Isn't he a charmer?"

"So handsome," Lucinda said. "May I hold him?"

"Of course. He's not the least bit shy around new people. In fact I suspect he likes a crowd. More attention for him."

Lucinda took the baby and cradled him in her arms. "Oh, little one. You look like your uncle. The same dark hair and blue eyes."

The baby smiled up at her and Lucinda smiled in

return. "You're going to be a heartbreaker. I can see it already. You're going to twist me around your finger, aren't you?" She returned her attention to Cynthia and the truck that had stopped in the driveway.

"Mr. Jonathan said you would be buying the little one what he needs." Reluctantly she handed the baby back to Cynthia. "After I show you around I'll go tell the men where to put everything. They're going to track mud all over my floors. I just know it." She glanced at the boxes and cartons of furniture being unloaded, then sighed. "It will be worth it, I think. To have a baby after all this time."

Lucinda motioned for Cynthia to follow her into the house. "Let me take you to the room I picked for the little one. Mr. Jonathan said I could just go ahead and choose what I think is best. I have a room for you, too. We had painters through last spring, so the rooms are nice. The baby's room is plain. Cream walls. But maybe we'll pick some wallpaper." She clucked Colton under his chin. "You like race cars? Or maybe sports?"

Lucinda continued to talk as she headed for a curved staircase at the far end of the foyer but Cynthia couldn't answer. She was too busy trying to keep her mouth from falling open as she took in her surroundings.

Of course she'd known that Jonathan Steele was a successful, wealthy man. Everyone in Grand Springs knew that. But reading about it in a newspaper article and seeing the proof in person were two very different things. She was sure she'd never seen a house as wonderful as this. Not even in a magazine spread.

The foyer was about the size of her mother's house, but oval instead of square. Above was an incredibly beautiful crystal chandelier and above that, a domed ceiling. The walls were white, the floor black-and-white marble. Gilded chairs that looked English and very old hugged the sides of the curved room. Molding added elegance to an already impressive entryway. There were a half-dozen doors leading to who knows what other wonderful rooms and a curved staircase that stretched up the far wall.

Cynthia continued to look around as she hurried after Lucinda.

"The bedrooms are all on this floor," Lucinda was saying when they reached the landing for the second story. "Mr. Jonathan's suite is at the back of the house. It's more private and quiet there. You and the little one are up here."

She turned right and walked along a long, carpeted corridor. Cynthia looked at the narrow occasional tables and the fresh flowers. There were paintings and mirrors and more doors leading to different rooms.

Lucinda walked through an open door on the left. Cynthia followed. "I had the furniture moved out yesterday and everything is clean," Lucinda said motioning to the impressive space. "There's a smaller room next door. I thought maybe for play now, and later as a place to study."

Cynthia slowly turned in a circle. The bedroom was huge, maybe fifteen-by-twenty, and on a corner of the house. There were windows on two walls, giving the area plenty of light. Hardwood floors gleamed underfoot. An arched doorway led to an alcove—the play or study area Lucinda had mentioned. There was also a private bath complete with a tub big enough to swim in.

"It's perfect," she breathed.

Colton gurgled his agreement, but his eyelids were

drifting closed and she knew he would be dozing in a matter of seconds.

Lucinda smoothed her apron and smiled. ''You like? It's big, but I thought as the baby grows, he will want the room. You're across the hall.'' She frowned. ''The walls and doors in this house are solid. I don't think you'll be able to hear the baby. Did you buy one of those walkie-talkies for baby?''

Cynthia shifted Colton to her other arm and nodded. ''A baby monitor? Yes. So I'll be able to hear him if he cries at night.''

''I would help,'' Lucinda said, ''but I don't live with Mr. Jonathan. I have a house of my own a few miles from here. Mr. Jonathan gave it to me when his father died and he moved back to the house. He said it was a gift for years of loyal service.'' She paused as the sound of a bell drifted through the house. ''The men from the truck. I'll be right back.''

She started to leave, then pointed to a closed door across the hall. ''That's your room. See if you like it.''

Cynthia did as she suggested. She crossed the carpeted hallway and pushed open the door. Her breath caught in her throat as she saw a feminine vision in pale blue and white.

Delicate French furniture filled the space that was only a little smaller than Colton's new room. The queen-size bed had been covered by a lacy spread. A triple mirror sat on top of a vanity table. Tall windows faced the front of the house and light poured through the lace curtains. There were two blue-and-cream striped wing chairs with a reading lamp between them and a small fireplace in the corner. The bathroom was just as lovely, with a tub as big as Colton's and an entire collection of bath products. She fingered the gold topped jars and figured the scented goodies cost as much as her mother spent on groceries in a month.

"What do you think?"

She turned at the sound of a male voice. Jonathan stood in the doorway of her bedroom. He wore a dark navy suit and red tie. The tailoring was perfect enough to emphasize his lean strength.

Her heart fluttered at the sight of him and her mouth went dry. She was grateful to be holding Colton. At least the baby gave her something to do with her hands.

"You have a beautiful house," she said sincerely. "It's big enough to serve as a shelter if there's a local emergency, but I'm not complaining."

Humor crinkled the corners of his blue-gray eyes. "I want you to be comfortable here."

"I think that's a given."

He glanced over his shoulder. Behind him Cynthia saw three men all carrying large boxes.

"It's an invasion," Jonathan said.

"I'm not sure about your choice of words, but there *is* a lot of stuff. Babies might be small but they have big needs. There's a crib and changing table, not to mention a dresser and playpen. You did say to start from scratch and get everything."

"I'm not complaining, Cynthia. I've never had any experience with a small child. I appreciate your expertise."

She nodded. "I was happy to help. I'll admit that I enjoyed the shopping, but I can't help wondering if it was all necessary. I don't mean to be insensitive, but your brother and his wife would have had a full nursery at their home. Didn't you want to use any of that furniture?"

His expression tightened and she knew she'd overstepped her bounds. "I'm sorry," she said quickly. "It's not my business."

"No need to apologize," he told her. "However I would prefer that my nephew had a fresh start here."

Which told her precisely nothing. Cynthia had the feeling that there was much she didn't know about Jonathan's relationship with his late brother. She wanted to ask, but then she reminded herself that she was just the hired help. It wasn't her job to get personally involved with the family.

"He'll need a few things from the house," she said, pressing the point because she knew it was important. "Favorite toys and some photos of his parents. Colton won't remember them but it's important for him to have a connection with his past."

Jonathan looked at the little boy dozing in her arms. "That's an excellent point. I'll make a note of it." He glanced at his watch. "Now if you'll excuse me, I've heard from the police that the bodies will be released Thursday. I came home from the office because I need to make arrangements for the funeral."

He spoke so matter-of-factly—as if he were simply working his way down a to-do list. But she didn't believe that for a second. Cynthia remembered the pain of having to make arrangements for her stepfather. Her heart went out to Jonathan. She took a step toward him.

"I know this is all difficult for you. If there's anything I can do, I'll be happy to help. It doesn't matter what you need. I mean that."

One corner of his mouth quirked up. "One or two things come to mind, but I doubt that is what you were thinking. So no, Cynthia. I'm fine. But I appreciate the offer."

She stared at him, not sure what he was talking about.

What could he want from her that she wouldn't be willing to do? If there were phone calls to make or details to be arranged, she would be happy to—

"How old are you?" he asked abruptly.

She frowned. "Twenty-six. Why on earth would you ask me that?"

"Because I could tell that my comment confused you. Which goes to prove my theory that you are much too innocent." His gaze traveled up and down her body. "And too young for me."

Now she was *really* lost. "Too young? Are you concerned about my abilities to take care of Colton?"

"Not at all."

"Then what…" Her voice trailed off. Realization came slowly but with great conviction. Sex? Were they talking about sex?

Even as heat flared on her face, she replayed the last bits of their conversation. Then she had to fight off a very clear visual of her and Jonathan stretched out in the bed not five feet from where they were standing. After that her imagination lost the ability to fill in the pieces, mostly because she'd never gone that far.

"Oh," she murmured, not able to meet his gaze. "I see."

"Don't worry," Jonathan told her. "You are now an employee of mine and I have a strict policy against sexual harassment. If I have to, I will fire myself."

That made her smile. She risked looking at him.

His expression was intense. "I mean it," he said. "I want you to feel safe here."

"I'm not worried." She wasn't. If anything she was intrigued. Did he really find her attractive in that way? He might think there was too much of an age difference between them but she didn't believe it for one second. "And I understand what you're saying."

"Are you sure?"

She hesitated, then shrugged. "Not really. I've never met anyone like you before."

"I'm aware of that." He raised his eyebrows. "You keep wanting to make me one of the good guys and I keep telling you that I'm not. You would do well to remember that, Cynthia. Heed my warning and you won't get hurt."

Jonathan had planned to spend the afternoon making arrangements for David and Lisa's funerals. However he found he couldn't concentrate with all the activity in the house. After the baby furniture was delivered, it had to be assembled. There were clothes to unpack and supplies to be put away. Lucinda interrupted him three times in less than fifteen minutes, the last time to show him a mobile of fuzzy jungle animals that spun gently to the music of a lullaby. Obviously the smell of baby powder had affected his housekeeper's brain.

So he returned to his office in downtown Grand Springs. At least he had more control in the steel-and-glass structure. He could inform his assistant that he didn't want to be disturbed and she would make sure no one interrupted him.

He walked into his office with the intention of telling her just that, but he didn't get the chance. Because when he pushed open the heavy glass doors that led to the Steele Enterprises executive suite, a tall, sultry brunette rose to her feet and smiled at him.

"Ms. Porter is here to see you," the receptionist behind the cherry wood desk said unnecessarily.

Martha Jean Porter glided across the thickly carpeted floor and smiled at him. "Hello, Jonathan."

Martha Jean was in her mid-thirties, with the perfect skin and wide green eyes of a classic beauty. She'd been turning men's heads since she was thirteen. Years of dance had given an already perfect body amazing posture and grace. She had the face of an angel, the body of a centerfold and the heart of a snake. She was his kind of woman.

"Martha Jean." He studied her simple black dress. It clung in all the right places, exposing enough cleavage to tempt a saint and legs long enough to be the envy of a racehorse. "I'm surprised to see you," he said ushering her into his private office. "You must be between husbands."

Her hips swayed as she walked. He found himself watching the movement with less interest than usual.

Martha Jean tossed her small leopard print handbag onto his desk, then sank onto the leather sofa in the corner. She patted the cushion next to her and smiled.

"Come sit next to me and I'll tell you all about the pitiful state of my marriage."

"So you're leaving Frederick?"

He put his briefcase next to her purse and joined her. She angled herself toward him and tucked a silky raven curl behind one shell-shaped ear.

"He's boring. Rich, but boring." She slid toward him and placed her hand on his thigh. "Why are you the only interesting, wealthy man I know?"

Her fingers had a familiar warmth. He and Martha Jean had played this game many times before. He picked up her hand and placed it on her own lap. "You know I don't want to get married. Not even for the privilege of being husband number four."

Full lips pouted. "I don't want to get married, either. I've learned my lesson." She paused to smile coyly. "At least until my money runs out. But that's far in the future. Frederick is going to be very generous. He had some very interesting…needs and he doesn't want me talking about them."

"You're blackmailing him." It wasn't a question.

"I'm advising him that I can be persuaded to keep quiet, but only under the right circumstances." She waved a manicured hand. "But that's not why I'm here." She gazed out the floor-to-ceiling windows. "It's almost winter. I thought we might discuss the possibility of keeping each other warm."

"A temporary liaison?"

"Exactly." She slid close. "You know how good we are together."

He couldn't dispute her comment. He and Martha Jean had been lovers on and off for several years. She knew more ways to keep a man happy in bed than any other woman he'd met. When she was between husbands, he found her a convenient diversion. She was beautiful, undemanding and knew how to behave in business and social situations. Best of all, she didn't pressure him for a commitment.

Talk about a perfect situation. He'd been celibate for far too long and there weren't any other likely candidates around. Jonathan preferred women who understood he wasn't interested in permanent anything. His recent attraction to the very innocent and inappropriate Cynthia Morgan warned him that he needed to do something to take care of his needs. Martha Jean was his answer.

Except…he couldn't seem to get excited about the thought of being with her. Even conjuring up memories of all the things they'd done in bed didn't help. When he looked into her perfect face, he saw a different pair of green eyes, ones that were more hazel. Instead of gleaming raven curls, he saw a blond braid.

Hell, she was haunting him. No woman haunted him. He didn't believe in it. "Why don't we meet to discuss terms," he said. "I can't do anything next weekend. I'll have to deal with my brother's funeral. Does the following Saturday work for you?"

Catlike eyes regarded him thoughtfully. "I'd hoped it could be sooner, but I suppose I can wait." She pressed her full, red lips together. "I heard about your brother, Jonathan. It's very sad, although you weren't close, so you can't be all that broken up about it."

She leaned forward, kissed him and rose to her feet. "I'll be in touch to work out the details."

He watched her leave. Nothing about her presence had aroused him. Which was unfortunate. He needed a distraction and Martha Jean was the safest one he knew. Her casual attitude about David's death matched his feelings on the subject but he couldn't help contrasting her pragmatic dismissal to Cynthia's heartfelt sympathy and pain.

She was a child, he told himself. All of twenty-six, with no experience in the world. He couldn't possibly be interested in her. There were too many years and miles between them. What would there be to talk about?

Yet it was *her* face, not Martha Jean's, that filled his mind when he tried to work, and her voice that kept drifting through his head. He vowed he would get his secretary right to work on finding a permanent nanny. Someone who would not be the least bit intriguing to him. Someone completely unlike Cynthia. In the meantime, he would simply avoid temptation by keeping as far away from her as possible.

Several days later Jonathan arrived home late. His first meeting of the day had been a working breakfast and the last had been a working dinner, with people in and out of his office all day long. Now, as he walked through the quiet house, he wondered how long he was going to have to stay away from his own home.

His plan wasn't turning out the way he'd thought. Even though he didn't see Cynthia, he still thought about her. If he didn't know it was physically impossible, he would swear that he could smell her light perfume drifting through the house.

Grumbling to himself, he made his way down the hall, stopping when he saw a light in the study. He crossed to the room and glanced inside.

Cynthia sat curled up in one of the leather chairs. A book lay open on her lap and she seemed genuinely caught up in the story. Jonathan took advantage of the moment to study her. She wore a sweatshirt over jeans, and white socks but no shoes. Her hair had started the day in a fancy braid, but now most of it had come loose and fluttered around her face. A faint frown pulled her eyebrows together and she nibbled on her bottom lip as she read.

Compared to Martha Jean, Cynthia was about as elegant as a milkmaid. Yet just looking at her was enough to get his blood pumping both hotter and faster. He wanted to step into the room and pull her into his arms. He wanted to bury himself inside of her until they were both slick with sweat and lost in passion. Worse, he wanted to *talk* with her. He wanted to hear about her day and tell her about his. He wanted to see what she thought of his latest deal. He didn't know her well enough to guess her opinions on most matters and the thought of finding that out tempted him.

It wasn't her, he told himself. It was because there was a woman waiting for him. He wasn't used to that. Lucinda had her own house and he didn't as a rule invite women to stay. So he usually came home to emptiness and silence.

"You're up late," he said.

Cynthia started, then looked up at him and smiled. "I didn't hear you come in." She closed the book. "How was your day?"

"Fine. Busy." He crossed to the leather sofa opposite her chair and sat.

The study had always been one of his favorite rooms in the house. It was also one of the few he hadn't renovated after his father's death. Bookshelves still lined three walls, their contents carefully catalogued on his computer. The desk opposite the fireplace was nearly two hundred years old and had been brought to Grand Springs by train nearly a century before. As a child he'd spent countless happy hours curled up in one of the leather chairs in this room, reading. Books had always allowed him to escape to a happier place than his home.

"I had a business dinner," he told her, not sure why he felt he had to explain where he'd been.

"Lucinda mentioned that." Cynthia pressed her fingertips against the top of the book. She drew in a deep breath and met his gaze. "I appreciate that you're very busy. Between your work and dealing with your brother's death, you haven't had a lot of spare time. But you've been gone since Friday. You get home late and leave early. You can't keep doing this. Colton needs you."

Until she'd mentioned the baby, he'd practically forgotten he existed. "Colton is a baby. What he needs is a nanny."

"He needs a father. Or at least an uncle who will become a father in time."

That was not information he needed to hear. "I'm not his father. Nor do I know how to fulfill the role." His own father had done a poor job raising him. Jonathan didn't want the past repeating itself. Even more, he didn't want to become involved with a child. Not this one or any one.

"You'll learn together," Cynthia said confidently. "It's just a matter of practice and love. But how are you going to get to know him enough to even like him, let alone love him, if you don't spend time with him?"

Love? "I don't want to love him," he said curtly. "What's the point?"

He thought she would get angry at his blunt statement, or contradict him. Women seemed to live to believe in love. In his mind, it was all a waste of time. But Cynthia surprised him. Instead of being upset, she simply set her book on the end table next to her and slid forward in her chair.

"Jonathan, I know thinking about David being gone is painful, but you have to push your grief aside enough to deal with your nephew. Right now it seems that there is no point in loving anyone. After all, once you love them they go away, right? You lost your mother when you were very young. Your father died a few years ago and now David is gone. But you still have Colton and if you let yourself get close to him, you'll find that you can help each other to heal."

She sighed. Her eyes focused on his face and he could practically touch the compassion and earnestness oozing from her. "I know that when you look at Colton you see David. That has to be painful now, but in time you'll appreciate the connection to your brother. You'll be happy that a piece of him lingers on. You can transfer the love you have for your brother to Colton. Love is very flexible that way. It bends and grows to fit the situation."

He couldn't believe what she was saying. Worse, he couldn't believe *she* believed it. Was she insane or just misguided?

"I don't know where you got your information," he told her, "but I'm not in mourning for my brother. I don't feel regret or even remorse that he's gone. I have no emotions. Only questions."

"I understand," she said. "You want to know who killed him."

He shrugged. "I have some mild curiosity about that, but I'm mostly concerned with why he was stealing from the company and why he hired someone to try to kill me. That poison you accidentally drank was compliments of him and intended for me."

# Chapter 6

"No," Cynthia said, vigorously shaking her head. "That's not possible."

Jonathan stared at her blandly, as if he'd just informed her about rain in the morning's forecast. He didn't look upset or angry. She couldn't have heard him correctly. That was it. He hadn't really accused his brother of trying to have him killed.

Jonathan leaned back in the sofa. He shifted so that his ankle rested on his opposite knee. Most of the light in the room came from the reading lamp by her right shoulder which meant that he was in shadow. His new position made it even more difficult for her to clearly see his face.

"It's more than possible," he said, his voice low, as if he were tired. "David and I—" He hesitated. "To say we didn't get along is putting it mildly. David always hated me. I never understood why. He was the favorite, he had every opportunity, but it wasn't enough.

About a year ago I realized that someone was stealing from the company. I had my suspicions but I didn't think David would be that stupid.''

"I thought he worked for you," she said, still trying to make sense of what he'd said. "Isn't the company partially his?"

"It was. Our father left us each ownership of different divisions. However, I had control over the day-to-day operations. David hated that."

"But if he stole from the company, he was stealing from himself."

"David wouldn't see it that way. He was only concerned about taking what I had. It was months before I figured out how he was doing it, and even longer to get proof. I confronted him at the party last week. I told him he had until morning to put the money back or I would have him arrested. But he didn't care. He said he was leaving the country and while he was gone, I would have a fatal mishap. Then he would own it all."

She stared at him. "I can't believe this."

"Not every family is like yours. Not everyone is good."

"I know that," she said defensively. "I'm not stupid."

"I think you're innocent. That's different from stupid." He shrugged. "The police found tickets to Rio in David's possession after he was killed. He'd meant everything he said."

Cynthia leaned forward. "I don't understand. How could you be so different? I don't want to speak ill of your brother, but he sounds like a horrible man. Yet you're so good."

"I've told you, I'm a bastard. You'd better learn that. As for us being different, we are that. I learned early that I had to work for what I wanted. I don't think David ever figured that out. He got used to taking what interested him, whether it was a toy, a business or a woman. In the end, he played out of his league and it cost him his life, along with his wife's.''

She pressed her lips together. If she believed what Jonathan told her—and he had no reason to lie—then the current situation here at the house started to make sense.

"So you're avoiding Colton because of his father. You're angry at David and angry at the baby.''

"So much for me being a saint,'' he said lightly.

"Oh.'' She touched her hand to her chest. "I didn't mean that in a bad way.''

"Of course not. It's quite a compliment.''

"Jonathan, no. It's a perfectly natural reaction.''

He gazed at her steadily. "I'm not angry with Colton, nor am I punishing him. I don't feel anything for him. Until the woman from child protective services showed up with him at your house a few days ago, I'd never seen the kid. I told you—David and I weren't close. I hadn't been to his house in years and I'd never met Colton. I'm not hostile, I'm just not interested.''

His words eased some of the tension inside of her. While she might not know how to handle the rest of Jonathan's situation, she knew how to deal with people who had never been around babies.

"It's just a matter of getting used to him,'' she said. "Give him a chance. He needs you, Jonathan. And I think you need him. Just try. Spend some time with him. Learn what it's like to be with him. I think you'll find you like it. Being a positive part of a child's life is the greatest joy in the world.''

She didn't have to clearly see his expression to know that he wasn't impressed with her argument.

"I don't share your love of family," he said flatly. "Most aren't as perfect as yours."

"Mine isn't perfect," she told him. "If it's good now, it's because everyone worked hard to make it that way." She pressed her lips together and wondered how she could convince him of the importance of making a choice.

"My mother got pregnant when she was fifteen," she began. "Her parents, my grandparents, were furious. My father ducked out on his responsibilities. He disappeared, never to be heard from again. When my mom turned eighteen, her still angry family threw her out. I was barely three."

She smiled wryly. "I don't remember much about that time in my life. My mom had to have been terrified. She had no skills, no support system and she was responsible for a toddler. But we grew up together. We were poor, I guess, but that wasn't important. My mom loved me and was there for me."

Warmth filled her along with the memories. "There were so many times she could have given up, but she didn't. She kept struggling and she kept us together. It was a conscious choice on her part. It's like when she married Frank. I could have decided that I wanted my mom all to myself and have made his life difficult. But I didn't. I chose to get to know him. And then I found out he was a wonderful man. I was lucky to have him in my life."

She shifted until she was sitting on the edge of her seat. "You are such an amazingly giving person, Jonathan. Your generosity has changed dozens of lives. By funding the seed money for new businesses, you give people a chance to make their dreams come true. You have such a big heart already. Can't you open it enough to let in a little baby boy?''

He sprang to his feet and paced to the fireplace. There, he braced one arm against the mantel. ''I don't know where you get off saying these things. You're nothing but a Pollyanna. You always see the best in people.''

She couldn't help laughing. ''You say that like it's a flaw.''

He spun to face her. ''Of course it is. People are not good or selfless. They're selfish bastards and they'll take you for everything you've got if you let them.''

''You want the world to think you're the big bad wolf, but the truth is, you're a softy, Jonathan Steele. You don't fool me for a minute.''

He stared at her. ''If you believe that, then you are a fool. Make no mistake—I'm capable of acting exactly like the wolf. I could rip you apart without even trying.''

She shook her head. ''Why do you want me to think the worst of you? What are you trying to hide?''

''I'm telling you the truth.'' He took a single step toward her. ''Don't challenge me, Cynthia. You can't win.''

She rose and moved to stand in front of him. ''This isn't meant to be a challenge. What are you afraid of? Why do you have to keep the whole world at bay?''

He tensed at her words. If she hadn't been watching, she might not have seen the sudden stiffness in his muscles. Somehow she'd reached the heart of the matter.

They were standing so close, she thought suddenly, caught by the fire in his eyes. She knew he was angry with her. There was an energy around him. She supposed she should have been afraid of him—after all he was Jonathan Steele and she knew nothing about him... Except what her heart told her. The instinct she'd always trusted said that he was a good man. A gentle man. That his hard nature was just a mask.

"Get out," he growled. "Get out before I do something we'll both regret."

Instead she took a step closer. "I'm not afraid."

He reached up and grasped her hair, holding her firmly at the base of her neck. "I can make you afraid. I can make you beg and plead for me to let you go."

She supposed he was trying to frighten her. But instead of fear, she found herself filled with a kind of heat. She'd only felt it once before and that had been while Jonathan had been kissing her at the ball.

"You can huff and puff all you want," she said softly. "I'm made of sterner stuff than that."

"Who the hell *are* you?" he demanded, but didn't give her time to answer. Instead he moved forward and, with his free hand, hauled her up against him.

"Run!" he demanded just before his mouth claimed hers. "Run away, little girl."

But she couldn't run. She couldn't move. She couldn't do anything but accept the fiery passion of his kiss as he claimed her mouth.

There was no delicate dance this time. He didn't ask or wait for permission. Instead he took what he wanted in a hard, hot embrace that left her shaken and breathless. His mouth moved over hers like a conquering hero claiming his spoils.

Cynthia didn't respond at first. She waited for the fear that must surely follow such an attack. She gathered herself to push away, to spring back, to do as he said...to run.

But she couldn't. Not because her body was frozen in place, but because she didn't want to. She'd been wishing he would kiss her again since the moment he stopped in the ballroom of the Grand Springs Empress Hotel. Even in the hospital, while she'd been recovering, she'd found her thoughts returning again and again to Jonathan's kiss and the feel of his body pressed against hers. Now that he was doing it again and she could inhale his scent and taste his masculine sweetness, she saw no reason to make him stop.

Despite what he tried to claim, she knew the truth. He *was* a good man. Honest, caring, and wounded inside. He couldn't have learned all he had about his brother without it having an impact on him. She ached for his pain. She wanted to heal him. She sensed that was one of the reasons he kissed her. Instinctively he reached out to another person to ease his pain.

Then his tongue brushed against her lower lip and she found that she couldn't think anymore. She couldn't do anything but absorb the sensations that crashed through her like the tide against the shore. Wave upon wave of passion made her quiver and question and wonder how this amazing thing could be happening to her.

She put her hands on his shoulders, then slowly parted her mouth. He groaned against her and swept inside, claiming her in a fit of desire that stole her breath. He explored her and teased her, touching, tasting, taking. He took and took and she continued to offer more. Because the more he needed, the more she seemed to have to give him. She strained to get closer, wanting to heal him with her passion.

Being like this with him felt so right. Need burned inside of her. A wanting she'd never experienced before. She knew the logistics of what happened between a man and a woman, but not the details. Suddenly she wanted to know everything, to experience it all in this man's arms.

His hand released her hair only to move up and down her back. Long, strong fingers learned the curves of her hips and then her rear. He cupped her there and hauled her up against him. Her belly flattened against him and she felt an unfamiliar ridge. Her inexperienced brain took several seconds to figure out what it was. Jonathan was aroused. Just by this relatively innocent kiss. He might find her young and annoying and a Pollyanna, but he still wanted her.

The information filled her with a lightness that made her wonder how she kept from floating away. She, Cynthia Morgan, virgin, had somehow captured this man's attention. She surged against him, shocking herself when she made her way into his mouth and began to explore him as he'd explored her. Instinctively she arched her hips toward him and moved her pelvis in a rhythm that provided counterpoint to the actions of her tongue.

Jonathan thrust her away and swore. His eyes were bright with fire, his breathing nearly as fast as hers. He still wore a suit from his day at the office. Now he loosened his tie and unfastened the first couple of buttons on his shirt.

"I won't apologize," he said, his voice low and challenging.

"Good. Because that would really annoy me." She had to clear her throat to make her voice sound right.

He stared at her, his gaze intense. Then he reached up and rubbed his thumb against her bottom lip. "I want you."

His words sent a thrill racing through her. Between

her legs, her muscles convulsed and she felt a sudden spurt of wetness on her panties.

"I—I want you, too," she managed to say, then had to duck her head so he wouldn't see her blush.

"The hell you do. You don't know the first thing about being with a man like me."

"I could learn."

He groaned and turned his back on her. "You're out of your league. You can't win this game."

"It's not a game and so far I'm holding my own." A flash of temper gave her courage. She walked around him until they were facing each other again. "You treat me like a child. Okay, I'm younger than you and I haven't lived a life similar to yours. Yes, I think the best of people. But I'm not simple and I'm not weak. When I was young, my mom was gone a lot, working. I grew up fast. I was responsible and capable at an age when most kids were still watching Saturday morning cartoons. When my stepfather died, I'm the one who held the family together. I've been a mature woman for a long time."

His gaze turned haunted. "Then why aren't you afraid of me?"

With that, he walked out of the room, leaving her alone with only the sound of her rapidly fluttering heart.

Cynthia flipped through the pile of bills she'd picked up on her visit to her office. She had a briefcase full of work, including several phone calls to return. It made sense to spend the morning at her office where she could work quickly and efficiently, but around ten-thirty, she found herself getting restless.

Now she walked up the front stairs to Jonathan's house and told herself that she was acting crazy. Why

had she returned here rather than staying at the headquarters of Mother's Helper? Several answers came to
her at once, but she didn't like any of them. Not the
one that said she wanted to be in Jonathan's house because being there made her feel as if she was closer to
him, nor the one that mentioned something about missing Colton and needing to feel the baby's warm weight
in her arms.

"You know better than to bond with a child," she
told herself sternly as she let herself in the front door.
"That's asking for nothing but trouble."

As for needing to be in Jonathan's house to feel
closer to him…she didn't have an answer for that, either.

"Lucinda, it's me," she called. "I'm back."

The housekeeper appeared at the top of the stairs. She
held the baby in her arms. "We were playing in his
room. He loves that big plastic truck you got him. You
know I always read about studies that say boys play
with cars and guns because that's what they're given,
but I think it's more than that. It's inside of them." She
tickled Colton's chin. "You're just a big boy who's
going to be a strong man, aren't you, sweetie?"

Colton waved his arms and giggled. He was always
happy, always loving, thriving on the attention showered on him by herself and Lucinda.

Cynthia glanced down at her suit. "I need to change
out of these clothes, then finish up the work I brought
home. Do you want me to take him, or—"

Lucinda cut her off with a quick wave. "I'll watch
him. You know I love to." She swung around in a wide
circle, holding out one of Colton's arms, as if they were
dancing. "I thought maybe I'd teach him the tango
later. Women love men who can tango."

Cynthia laughed as she made her way up the stairs. Lucinda was a wonderful addition to Jonathan's household and she hoped he understood what a treasure he had in her.

She passed the older woman and the baby still tangoing, then made her way into her bedroom. In a matter of minutes she'd changed into jeans and a sweater, then she sat down at the small desk by the window. An hour later she'd finished paying her bills, had updated her accounts and made most of her phone calls.

With most of her work nearly finished, Cynthia found that her mind started to wander. For one thing, she couldn't help remembering all that had happened the night before. Not just the kiss, although that had been amazing enough to keep her up most of the night. Being in Jonathan's arms had been as wonderful the second time as it had been at the ball.

She was still surprised that he didn't frighten or intimidate her. Maybe it was because she'd come close to death and didn't want to waste any time. Maybe it was because she had the strong feeling that she was the only one who really saw the truth inside of him. At least she had no regrets about what they'd done the previous night, or if she did, they were regrets that he'd stopped.

She'd never made love with a man. To be honest, she hadn't thought about it one way or the other. But being with Jonathan like that had made her think about the possibilities.

But as much as she reveled in being with him and however much she wanted to blush at the memory of her own boldness, what she couldn't escape was what he'd said about his brother. That David had stolen from the company and then had tried to kill him.

She squeezed her eyes shut as pain swept through

her. Pain for what Jonathan must be feeling. She couldn't imagine a brother acting like that. Even though she knew families weren't perfect and people didn't always love the way they should, David's actions were inconceivable.

With that new information, she completely understood Jonathan's resistance to Colton. On the one hand, Jonathan was fair enough to want to give the innocent child a chance, but on the other, he couldn't forget who the baby's father was. She knew now that it was her job to help Jonathan make peace with his past. She would have to help him see that Colton was as much a victim as he was and that together they could heal each other.

A soft knock interrupted her thoughts. Lucinda came in with a tray of coffee and sandwiches. "It's lunch. You didn't eat much at breakfast, so I knew you'd be hungry. I already gave Colton his bottle. He's about out for his nap."

Cynthia took the offered food. "Thanks, Lucinda," she said, smiling at the housekeeper. "You're too good to me."

The older woman shrugged. "You're easy. And at least I have something to do now. Mr. Jonathan is never home. He never entertains, nothing."

Cynthia thought about her questions and wondered if Lucinda would help. "Did you work here before Jonathan's father died?"

Lucinda sat in one of the wing chairs and nodded. Her short, dark curls bobbed with the movement. "I've worked here nearly fifteen years. Old Mr. Steele hired me. Mr. David was still at home on school holidays, but Mr. Jonathan was gone."

Cynthia hesitated. "Jonathan told me that he and his brother didn't get along."

Lucinda snorted in disgust. "Mr. David was a bad seed. I know we're not supposed to speak ill of the dead, but if anyone deserved it, it's him. Always in trouble, that one. And his father just looked the other way. Mr. Jonathan worked hard, he did great things with the company, but old Mr. Steele never noticed. Nothing was good enough. Mr. Jonathan is brilliant with the businesses, but did his father say even one kind word? No."

She paused, then pressed her lips together. "Mr. Jonathan loved this house. His father knew that, yet he left it to Mr. David. I never understood why. I was so angry. I told Mr. David I was quitting. I wouldn't work for him. Always with the parties and the women, that one. Even after he married, there were women." Her gaze narrowed. "Mr. David, he laughed at me and told me not to worry. That as soon as he took title of the property, he would be selling it back to his brother."

She leaned forward and lowered her voice. "I overheard Mr. David on the phone with his lawyer. He did what he said, but he charged Mr. Jonathan twice what the house was worth. And Mr. Jonathan paid it, too. Because he loved this house more than anything. I told him I was happy to work for him, so he kept me, too."

Cynthia didn't know what to say. Everything was so confusing. "I didn't know it could be like that between brothers."

Lucinda nodded. "I know. It's terrible. I never liked Mr. David, but Mr. Jonathan is different. Sometimes I think he is very sad inside. Like his heart is broken. I tell him to get married, to have babies. They will make him feel better. But he tells me I'm a romantic and it isn't that easy."

She rose to her feet and shrugged. Her expression turned shrewd. "Maybe now he'll listen, eh?"

"I think he and Colton can help each other," she said.

"Oh, yes, the baby. But that is not what I was thinking."

She winked and left before Cynthia could respond.

Once she was gone, Cynthia sat alone in her room and thought about what Lucinda had told her. There was so much pain in Jonathan's past. No wonder he resisted making emotional connections. Yet all his actions spoke for themselves. He saw what was right and he did it. Whether that meant helping out in the community, or worrying about her while she was in the hospital. When she looked at him she saw a strong man, but one who was very alone. Her heart ached for him.

She stood and quickly left her room. Across the hall, Colton's door stood open. She stepped inside and crossed over to the crib standing in the center of the room.

The baby wasn't quite asleep. He opened his eyes at her approach, then smiled broadly when he spotted her. Big blue eyes crinkled with laughter. Fat arms waved as he silently asked to be picked up.

"No, you don't, young man," she said softly. "It's your nap time. I'm just stopping by because I haven't seen you all morning and I'm a sucker for a handsome face like yours."

She touched his cheek, then his hand. His pudgy fingers closed around one of hers. As his grip tightened, so did a thin band encircling her heart. She knew she was in trouble. Bad enough to fall for the uncle, but far worse to fall for the child, as well. If she let herself care too much, when it was time to leave, she would find herself broken in two.

# Chapter 7

Jonathan arrived home the following Wednesday at four. He told himself that his earlier than usual arrival had nothing to do with a vague sense of guilt brought on by Cynthia's comments about his relations—or lack thereof—with his nephew. If he wanted to leave the office before his usual time, that was his prerogative. After all, he ran Steele Enterprises.

But as he pulled his car into the wide, five-car garage, he knew that he was lying. Even though he'd tried to ignore everything she said, he couldn't forget her words. While he had no interest in Colton, he didn't want to repeat the sins of *his* father. He remembered what it had been like growing up in a house where his only blood relative loathed the sight of him.

He entered the house and tried to figure out what he was going to say to Cynthia. Unfortunately his actions were going to add to her conviction that he was one of the good guys. He would have thought their last time together would have cured her of that, but she was nothing if not perverse.

The foyer was quiet and empty—usual occurrences for the large house. It had been many years since these walls had heard much in the way of laughter. But even as he registered sadness at the thought, he heard a faint sound from upstairs.

He climbed the stairs. The sound turned into singing, accompanied by many high-pitched squeals. Jonathan followed the noise into Colton's room and from there into the bathroom. He found Cynthia standing by the long vanity. She supported Colton, who sat in a small, blue, plastic tub. A small tape player stood on the closed toilet lid and she sang along with several high-pitched voices. The tape had been made for children but she seemed to know all the words.

Although her back was to him, Jonathan could see her clearly in the mirror. She wore her blond hair in a ponytail high on the top of her head. A damp white T-shirt clung to her chest, outlining her full breasts. She wasn't wearing any makeup, but her skin was lightly flushed from the warm water.

Colton squealed again. Cynthia looked down at him and smiled. Jonathan saw the softness in her expression, the tender curve of her mouth. He briefly wondered if his mother had ever bothered to look at him like that and decided that even if she had, the feelings must have faded, because she'd managed to walk out on him without ever once looking back.

Cynthia glanced up and saw his reflection in the mirror. Her smile broadened. "Now you know how I fill my day," she said. "It's not exactly the same world as high finance or whatever it is you do, but I like it."

Her jeans were a faded shade of blue and they hugged

her hips and thighs with a thoroughness he'd been intent on himself the other night. He still remembered how her rear had felt when he'd cupped it. Firm yet yielding. He'd wanted to peel off her clothes and feel that bare part of her.

"Are you really just twenty-six?" he asked abruptly, knowing that he wasn't going to like the answer.

"Of course." She grinned. "Hey it could be worse."

He winced. "You're practically jail bait. I'm thirty-seven."

"I know." Laughter danced in her eyes. "You kiss pretty good for an old man."

He knew she was teasing, but the phrase definitely hit below the belt. "You kiss pretty good for someone barely out of her teens."

"How rude," she said indignantly. "Is this where I remind you that I've been legal for several years now? In fact after college I actually left Grand Springs and made my way to the big city."

She lifted Colton out of the bath and placed him on a fluffy towel she had waiting beside the basin. When the baby was securely wrapped, she cradled him in her arms and walked back into the bedroom.

"What big city would that be?" he asked.

"Chicago. After college I had a job with an advertising firm there. They considered me 'high potential' and I was within a couple of months of getting on their management fast track when Frank was injured."

The humor fled her face as she set the baby on the changing stand. She dried him off as she spoke. "Then I came home and left all that behind. So you see, I'm not the hick you think."

"Okay, you had a whole year in Chicago. But you live at home now."

"Only because it's easier for my mom. We've been talking lately that it's time for me to get back out on my own. She has things pretty much under control."

"Will you go back to Chicago?"

She shook her head. "My life is here now. I enjoyed my time away but I'm not really that much of a city girl. I like Grand Springs. I learned that I want to be close to my family." She reached for a diaper and secured it around Colton's behind.

Jonathan leaned against the door frame and folded his arms over his chest. "Do you regret what you gave up? It sounds like you were on your way with the advertising firm."

She looked at him. "I don't regret a minute of it. When Frank was dying, he asked me to help out my mom. I would have done it anyway, but even if that hadn't been part of my plan I would have dropped everything to honor his request. He'd given me so much over the years. He was both surrogate father and big brother to me. I loved him and I'll always miss him. Being home made me feel closer to him."

She spoke with a sincerity he couldn't help believing. But even as he heard the words, he dismissed them. Mostly because he couldn't relate to what she was saying. How could anyone inspire that much devotion? It didn't make sense.

"After a few months I got the idea of starting my own business," she said. She opened one of the drawers below the changing table and pulled out a one-piece jumper thing. Despite Colton's attempts to squirm away, she expertly dressed the baby with practiced ease.

"You're good at what you do," he said, wondering how it was possible for something as small as a baby to grow into an adult.

"I love my work," she admitted. "And you're the reason I had the opportunity to get it all started."

He groaned. "Don't go there. I'm not in the mood for the saint speech."

"All right." She picked up the dressed baby and settled him in her arms, facing Jonathan. "That's your uncle," she told Colton. "Can you say Uncle Jonathan?"

Colton blew a raspberry instead. Cynthia laughed. "He won't be talking for a few more months, but he'll get there."

Jonathan stared at the infant. He could see some of his brother in the child's features. Or maybe he was seeing his own father instead. He stiffened slightly as he realized that for all his faults, David had managed to create a family for himself. He'd married Lisa and had had a baby. Someone to carry on his name and the legacy of the Steele family.

"How is he adjusting?" he asked, pointing at the baby.

"Not bad, considering." Cynthia nuzzled the top of his head. "He's a sweetheart. Some babies only bond with their parents and don't take to anyone else easily, but Colton is open to attention from all comers. He's very good-natured and healthy. The kind of baby who is easy to love."

Love. Something else Jonathan didn't believe in. Love was dangerous. It too easily turned to hate and vindictiveness. Marriage and children had never been a part of his plan. His cold, empty childhood had told him he never wanted to put any innocent baby through the same kind of hell he'd endured. Watching whatever feelings his father had had for him and his mother turn to anger and loathing had taught him that no love lasted very long.

"Do you want to hold him?" Cynthia asked, holding out Colton.

Jonathan straightened and took a step back. "No."

"You're going to have to do it sometime."

"That's what I pay you for."

She wrinkled her nose at him, then turned her attention to Colton. "Uncle Jonathan is very stubborn. Can you say stubborn?"

Her question earned her a faint smile.

Jonathan ignored the exchange. He turned to leave, then paused. "The funeral is Saturday. You said Colton should be there. You still think that?"

"Yes. He won't remember it, but when he's older he'll want to know that he was there."

"It's at one in the afternoon."

"We'll be ready."

"You don't have to go. Lucinda will be there."

"I don't mind," she told him. "I want to be there for both of you."

He almost didn't believe her. After all, her comment implied a form of caring. But then he reminded himself that this was Cynthia he was talking about and caring was the one thing she did best.

One day she would learn that being that soft was going to make her life hell. He only hoped that he wasn't the one to teach her that lesson.

The hillside graves stood side by side. Cynthia swallowed the tears burning her eyes and the back of her throat. She didn't cry for Lisa and David Steele—after all she'd never met the couple. Instead her sadness came from memories of Frank's funeral and the realization that Colton would never know his parents.

She hugged the baby closer to her. Colton responded with a cooing sound that eased some of the ache in her heart.

"Are you all right?" Jonathan asked softly from his place beside her.

"I'm fine. Anyway, I'm supposed to be asking *you* that question. How are you holding up?"

He shrugged. "Fine."

The funeral service ended and people made their way to the graveside for the final words from the minister. Cynthia glanced at the gathering crowd. It was a cool early November afternoon. Although the sky was clear, the temperature had been dropping for days.

Everyone was appropriately dressed in black for the occasion, but Cynthia saw few signs of real sorrow. No woman wept, no man looked stricken. From what she could tell, the polite collection of people was of mostly business associates. There was no family save Jonathan and Colton, and few friends.

At the church service she'd noticed that most people who had spoken had done so in the abstract, as if they hadn't really known David or Lisa.

"Where are his friends?" she asked in a low voice.

Jonathan glanced down at her. "I'm not sure he had any. I wouldn't have known them. David was seven years younger than me. When we were growing up we were always at different places in our lives."

Cynthia nodded, then looked at Lucinda. The housekeeper had a faint frown pulling her eyebrows together. Cynthia remembered all that she'd said about David. None of it had been flattering.

How could two brothers have been so different, she wondered. How could they have become so estranged?

The minister began to speak. She listened to his words. Colton was quiet as if the baby recognized the solemnity of the occasion. Now he and Jonathan only had each other. Cynthia vowed that she would make sure they bonded together to form a family unit. After all that he had been through, Jonathan deserved someone to love, who loved him back.

David Steele's house was as coldly modern as Jonathan's was old-fashioned and welcoming. Both were huge and expensive. While during the dark of night Cynthia could play a silly game of pretend and actually see herself settling permanently in Jonathan's home, David's place of residence seemed to mock her from the moment she entered the front door.

Huge white walls soared up two stories, broken only by splashes of color provided by large canvases of confusing modern art. In the center of the massive foyer stood a fat white marble column topped by a slick, black grinning creature—part gargoyle, part devil. The white tile floor made the open area seem even bigger and Cynthia had the feeling that if she spoke, her voice would echo.

Jonathan moved through an archway into another room. She followed and found herself in an open living area. There were huge windows with views of the city and the mountains beyond. Here the color scheme was again predominantly white with only the artwork providing any contrast.

"The view must be something at night," she managed to say by way of a comment. What she wanted to say was that she'd never been in a place that made her feel so incredibly cold.

"From what I remember, it's very impressive," Jonathan said. "I've only been here a couple of times before."

Cynthia shivered. At least she'd thought to have Lucinda take Colton home after the funeral. She hated to think of that bright, happy baby in this ice palace.

Jonathan turned slowly in the center of the living room. "I don't know why I bothered to come here. There's nothing that I want."

Cynthia sighed. "I know you feel that way now, and it makes sense. After all, you and David were hardly close. But time may change your opinion of him, or at least blunt some of your anger. If you don't take a few mementos now, when you can, you may regret it."

"So speaks Pollyanna," he grumbled. "You could find good in the devil."

"That would be a stretch even for me." She looked at the sculpture of a wounded bull at the feet of a bullfighter and shuddered. "But I still stand by what I said. Also, we need to pick up some pictures for Colton to have later. And I want to look at his room here. There might be a few things we should take back to your house." Although she couldn't imagine it right now.

Jonathan didn't say anything. Instead he led the way back into the foyer and up the stairs to the second floor. In the white-on-white master bedroom, she saw pictures scattered along a marble-topped dresser. They were all of David and Lisa. Not a single photo showed Colton. Cynthia frowned at the oversight.

"Take whatever you want," he said. "I'll go down to the kitchen and get some bags so we can carry the stuff out."

She nodded, then began to study the framed snapshots. There was David and Lisa on vacation in different parts of the world, a couple of wedding pictures and some candid shots of them around the house. She picked three at random, then added one of the wedding photos. Next, she went down the hall until she found a study.

There were books and a desk large enough to serve as an alternate runway for the local airport. Several of the bookshelves held framed pictures. She walked over and began to study them.

She was looking at a picture of David with an older man when Jonathan entered the room. "Is this your father?" she asked.

He walked over to stand next to her. "Yeah."

On another shelf she found pictures of the older man with a pretty woman. "Your mother?"

Jonathan shook his head. "David's mother. My stepmother." He shrugged. "She was good to me. I missed her when she died."

There weren't any pictures of Jonathan in the room. But then how many brothers kept pictures of each other standing around? She collected a half-dozen more pictures and added them to the bags Jonathan had found.

"At least you had one positive family experience," she said lightly. "Your stepmother. Did you get along with your father?"

The question popped out before she could call it back. Too late she remembered what Lucinda had said about Jonathan's relationship with the elder Mr. Steele.

His already tense expression tightened. "Not really."

She leaned against the desk. "But he had to have loved you and been proud of you, even if he didn't show it. Look at what a success you've made of yourself. From what I understand Steele Enterprises was a company going nowhere until you took it over. You turned everything around. He had to respect that.''

"You'd think," Jonathan said, avoiding her gaze. He walked over to a picture of David with his father. "I guess he appreciated what I could do with the company because he left me in charge. Even my dad had to see that David would only run it into the ground. But I don't think he respected me."

"He loved you," she said firmly. "Sometimes parents have trouble showing it, but he felt it."

"Did your mother's family love her?" he asked without turning around. "Is that why they threw her out when she was eighteen? Is that why you never see them?"

"I, ah..." She stared at his broad back, at the dark wool of his suit jacket. "How do you know I don't see them?"

"You never mention them." He faced her again. "I can read between the lines. They cut her off without a cent and they've never tried to reconcile. Knowing the little I do about your mother, I'm going to guess she made the attempt a couple of times, but they're not interested."

All the blood seemed to rush from her head. Every word he spoke was true. "How did you know that?"

"It wasn't hard to figure out." He shoved his hands into his slacks pockets. "Families are an invention of the devil. We're better off going it on our own. That way no one gets hurt."

"And no one gets loved. You can't want that."

"Love is an excuse to cause pain."

He spoke flatly, then grabbed the bag of photos and

left the room. "If you want to look at Colton's room, do it now. I want to get out of here."

She heard his footsteps on the stairs.

Cynthia stood in the center of the study for a long moment, then moved in the opposite direction Jonathan had taken. She pushed open doors until she found one that led to a baby's room. Except this wasn't like any child's room she'd seen before. Instead of being warm, welcoming and filled with homey furniture, she felt as if she was staring at a set decorated for a photo shoot.

Pale raw silk covered the walls and hung by the windows. The canopied crib looked both imposing and uncomfortable, the fabric matching the light cream color of the walls. Personal furnishings on the dresser were silver and glass. Although the décor wasn't as stark as the other rooms, there wasn't anything soft about the furniture or the decorations. No fuzzy stuffed animals littered the carpeted floor or corners. In fact there weren't any toys anywhere. It wasn't a baby's room at all—it was a showpiece.

"Do you want anything?"

She turned at the sound of the voice and saw Jonathan standing in the doorway. Apparently he'd changed his mind about going downstairs.

She motioned to the room. "I can't figure out if Colton had a lucky escape, or if I did his room all wrong."

His dark gaze stared past her, but she saw the bleakness in his expression. She wanted to go to him and have him hold her. She wanted them to kiss and touch and even make love. She wanted to be with him—both to heal and because he made her feel things she'd never felt before. But he was Jonathan Steele and she was just a nanny. She had no place in his world. He spent most of their time together trying to scare her off.

"What are you thinking?" he asked suddenly.

She glanced at him. "That you're a trial by fire. Knowing you is going to make me stronger."

"Or you'll get burned. If I were you, I wouldn't take odds on getting out unscathed."

Jonathan had stopped pretending to work about an hour before, but he didn't leave his study. He knew what awaited him out in the rest of the house—Cynthia. She and Colton lurked in the hallways, waiting to pounce, to claim his attention. She'd been hovering ever since they returned from David's house. He almost wished he had somewhere to go that night so he could escape her concern.

Except, if he was completely honest with himself, he didn't want to be anywhere but with her.

He swore under his breath, then picked up the paper Lucinda had left on his desk that morning. Maybe reading about the day's events would distract him.

But before he could get interested in a single article, he heard the doorbell ring. Seconds later a burst of laughter drifted through the big, lonely house. Conversation wafted back to him, along with more laughter.

Against his better judgment, he left his study and started toward the front of the house. He came to a halt in the doorway to the foyer. Jenny, Brad and Brett were skating on the slick marble. Their in-line skates glided easily over the floor as they circled around each other with casual grace.

Cynthia shrieked from midway down the stairs. "Are you insane? You can't skate in the house. Stop it now!"

"Ah, Cyn," one of the boys grumbled as all three of them slowed and looked up at her. "It's too cool in here."

"It's Mr. Steele's house. I don't even want to think about what kind of marks you're leaving on the floor."

"Lucinda said it was all right," Jenny said even as she plopped on the floor and started unfastening her skates. The teenager smiled at his housekeeper. "I don't think we left any marks but if we did, I'll help you clean them."

Lucinda leaned against the closed front door and waved away her comment. "I'll be fine. Mr. Jonathan doesn't make any kind of mess and I've been here for years. So you would have to do a lot of messing up to make up for how clean he is."

Jenny laughed, but the boys looked confused.

"We missed you," Jenny told her sister. She stood in her stocking feet. "So we skated over to see you." She scampered up the stairs. "How is little Colton?"

She cooed over the baby and then carefully took him in her arms. Brad and Brett scrambled to their feet. "So is there like a pool and stuff?" one of them asked.

Leaving the baby with Jenny, Cynthia made her way down the stairs and hugged the boys close. "I don't, like, know."

Both boys laughed. "Why do you hate it when we say 'like?'"

"It's not correct English. I want you to grow up to speak well."

"Do you think Mr. Steele has video games?" the other brother asked.

Jonathan watched the exchange. He noticed that Jenny had brought Colton downstairs and was standing close to her sister. Neither of the boys had moved out of Cynthia's embrace. They stood there, the Morgan children, so alike with their blond hair. Everyone wore sweatshirts and jeans. Even though Cynthia was exactly twice Jenny's age, she didn't look out of place with her sister or the boys.

They were her half siblings, he thought. Related in the same way he and David had been related. There was an even bigger age gap, yet somehow they had become a family. His chest tightened slightly as he wondered where he and his brother had gone wrong.

Lucinda bustled into the center of the room. "It's getting late," she said. "I think you should stay to dinner. I can cook many good things."

"That's great," one of the boys said.

Jonathan wondered if there was a way to tell the twins apart. He would have to ask Cynthia.

"I don't think that's a good idea," Cynthia said. "Mr. Steele doesn't want an invasion of my relatives disturbing his evening."

All three kids sent up a chorus of protests. Lucinda joined in, loudest of all.

"I don't think he'd mind," he said, speaking for the first time since arriving on the scene.

Five pairs of eyes focused on him. Cynthia blushed. "Oh. I thought you were still in your study. Sorry about this," she said, motioning to the crowd around her. "They came by to see me for a few minutes, but they were just leaving."

"There's no need for them to go if they don't want to," he told her. He turned his attention to the children. "Lucinda is a great cook, but I don't keep her busy enough. Why don't you three go on into the kitchen and see what she has in the cupboards and freezer, then you can pick something good for dinner."

Jenny and the boys didn't need to be asked twice. Jenny handed Colton to her sister, then sped after the other three as they walked across the foyer and through the far door.

Cynthia looked at him. "Why are you doing this?"

"Because I think you miss your family and they miss you. Oh, why don't you give your mom a call and invite her over as well. Unless she has plans."

An emotion flickered in her eyes. One that told him she thought he was a good man—despite all he'd told her about himself. He opened his mouth to protest her feelings, then closed it. For reasons he wasn't about to examine he found he liked that Cynthia thought the best of him. Even if it was just for the night.

# Chapter 8

Cynthia was still laughing as she walked from the dining room into the kitchen. She set the dirty dishes she'd been carrying on the counter, then paused as her mother followed her into the room.

"Your two boys are impossible," she said cheerfully.

"Hey, I don't deserve all the blame," Betsy said with a grin. "They're your brothers."

"It's not the same thing at all."

Betsy put her dishes next to Cynthia's, then turned in a slow circle as she took in the big kitchen. "Nice."

Cynthia followed her gaze, also admiring the granite countertops, the professional size stove and built-in refrigerator.

"The rich really are different," she told her mother. "Fortunately Jonathan isn't one to flaunt his wealth. I don't worry about feeling out of place here. Lucinda does her best to make me feel at home as well, and as you can tell, she's a great cook."

"No kidding. I thought I was good at whipping things up at the last minute, but she's a real pro."

Cynthia had to agree. In the time it had taken for Betsy to be invited over for dinner, then to arrive, Lucinda had thrown together an enchilada casserole and salad, frosted a two layer cake she'd baked the previous day and set the table.

Betsy began to load the dishwasher. "I'm glad you're adjusting to being here," she said. "You haven't taken an in-home assignment in a few months."

"I know." Cynthia collected dessert plates and forks. "I'd forgotten how much fun I have with the babies. Colton is a sweetie and I'm really enjoying my time with him. Lately I've been so caught up in the details of running my business that I've missed out on the hands-on part of what I do."

"That's what happens when you become a tycoon," her mother teased.

"I wish. Jonathan's the tycoon. I'm barely starting out."

Betsy straightened. She tucked a strand of hair behind her ear. In her jeans and sweatshirt she didn't look much older than Cynthia. "You seem to be getting along with Jonathan as well."

"He's been great."

Her mother sighed, then leaned against the countertop. "I know that you're a mature adult and you have to make your own decisions, but I can't help worrying about you where he's concerned. He seems like a nice man. He was so good to us while you were in the hospital, but..." Her voice trailed off.

Cynthia busied herself with finding more paper napkins. She had a feeling she knew what her mother was going to say and she didn't want to hear it.

"You have to remember who he is," Betsy finished at last.

Cynthia set down the package of napkins and faced her mother. "What happened to me believing in myself and doing my best? Didn't you always tell me I was just as good as anyone else?"

"Of course, and I still believe that, but that was a general comment and we're dealing with specifics where Jonathan is concerned." Betsy raised her hands, palms up, in a gesture that was both conciliatory and pleading. "I don't want you to get hurt. Jonathan is a fantasy man in your life. You've been so busy with helping me and starting your business that you haven't had much time to date. Looking back I see that I deserve a lot of the blame. I've leaned on you too much. But now I'm afraid you're going to look at Jonathan with all your pent-up longing and see him as what you want him to be, rather than what he is."

Cynthia forced a smile even though she wasn't sure how successful she was in the execution. "Jonathan keeps telling me the same thing. That I see him as a nice guy, but he's really a bastard."

Betsy looked startled at the comment. "I wouldn't go that far. I'm just pointing out that while to you he's a knight in shining armor, to him, you're his nephew's nanny. You are my daughter and I think you're amazingly special, but I'm not sure you're someone he would fall in love with. I'm only concerned about protecting you." She paused. "Does that make sense?"

Cynthia nodded slowly. "More than I want it to."

She hated thinking about her mother's words, but she knew they were wise and she would be a fool to ignore them. Whatever attraction might exist between her and Jonathan, it had no basis in reality.

But even as she thought that, a voice in her head whispered that the passion had been extraordinary, and she hadn't been the only one to think so. Jonathan had been aroused when they'd kissed. Of course men got aroused all the time and did it necessarily mean anything?

"Jonathan is going through a difficult time right now," her mother said. "He's just lost his brother and sister-in-law and has a new baby in his life. You are the one person rescuing him. But when things settle down, he's not going to need you so much."

"I know, Mom," she said. "Everything is really confusing right now, but I'll remember what you said. I know you want to keep me safe from harm." She hesitated. "I don't blame you for my lack of social life. I'm the one who chose to stay home."

Betsy regarded her thoughtfully. "I think it's time that changed. We have to learn to live without you and you have to get back to your own life."

"I agree."

But the thought of moving out made her sad. She'd enjoyed being with her family on a daily basis. Still, the natural order of things said that the young grew up and left. Circumstances had changed the course of her life—possibly for the better. Now it was time to tackle her own destiny.

Did that mean Jonathan? Or should she listen to her mother and assume that nothing between them was going to work? As much as she believed Betsy's words and knew that if she continued to think about him and long for him, she was bound to get hurt, she wasn't convinced she could simply turn her back on the man. Certainly not while she was living in his house. And she had no intention of leaving anytime soon. They hadn't begun to make plans for him to hire a permanent nanny.

But Jonathan kept telling her that he wasn't a prize— that if she wasn't careful, she was going to get hurt. Her mother's words reminded her that it might be prudent to listen. After all, he might just be telling the truth.

Jonathan looked up as Cynthia returned to the dining room. She carried a fancy cake on a plate. Betsy followed with plates and forks.

"I know the boys don't really like dessert," Betsy said in a playfully serious tone of voice. "You don't have to cut any for them."

Brad, or maybe it was Brett, slapped his hands flat on the table. "Mo-om, you know that's not true. We love dessert. Especially cake." He turned to Jonathan. "Did Lucinda bake it herself?"

"Sure. She bakes lots of things. There are probably enough frozen cookies in the freezer to open a bakery."

The boy's eyes widened at the thought. "Wow. Cookies in the freezer. Mom makes them all the time, but there aren't any left over to freeze. If there were, we could take 'em in our lunch."

"Imagine," Betsy teased. "But that would mean eating less when they were straight from the oven."

"Or you could bake more," her son offered.

"I suspect there will be leftover cake," Cynthia said as she started to cut into the flowered confection. "I doubt that Mr. Steele will mind if you take some home."

Both boys turned their attention to him. "Feel free," he said and earned two blazing smiles.

"Just a little piece," Jenny said from her seat across

the table. As she had at her own house, she held Colton in her arms. "The same size as yours, Cynthia."

Jonathan had noticed that Jenny was content to be her older sister's shadow, doing whatever she did, the same way at the same time. Brad and Brett obviously cared about their sister, but they didn't emulate her. Instead he'd caught them giving him worshipful glances from time to time.

"Do you think we could go look at your cars?" one of the boys asked. "We read this article about you a while back and it said you had a five-car garage and that it was filled." He spoke with a reverence only possible when male soon-to-be drivers discussed cars.

Jonathan chuckled. "Sure. After we finish dinner."

"Until then, leave Mr. Steele alone," Cynthia said, sliding a slice of cake in front of him.

Since the funeral and the visit to his brother's house, she'd changed out of her black dress into more casual attire. Her hair was still back in the fancy braid she favored. She looked impossibly young and beautiful.

He looked around at the table still covered with serving dishes from dinner. He tried to remember the last time he'd used the dining room for anything but a solitary dinner. Lucinda lamented his nearly monastic social life and his refusal to entertain. She'd been in her element this afternoon and evening as she'd prepared for his guests. No doubt when she returned on Monday she would lecture him to have people in more often.

At the far end of the table Brad and Brett had started a heated conversation about the virtues of a turbocharged V-6 engine versus a basic V-8. Jenny was busy telling them that cars were boring while Cynthia joined in to point out that they were all years from driving and wasn't there something else they could talk about.

Betsy, seated on his left, leaned forward. "Were you this interested in cars when you were their age?"

"Probably. I think most boys can't wait to be old enough to drive."

She nodded and looked at her sons. "They're growing up so fast. I can't believe they're already ten." She smiled. "Double digit ages are very important."

"Maybe at ten. They're less interesting now."

"I couldn't agree more," she said.

He looked at her, at the wide eyes so like her daughter's, at the ready smile. Betsy and Cynthia had a lot in common, although the mother had more wariness in her expression. It was hard to believe that she was only a few years older than himself and that she'd been a mere two years older than Jenny when she'd had Cynthia.

"They miss their father," Betsy said, nodding at the twins. "That's why they're clinging to you. Don't panic, they're not expecting a substitute, it's just that they don't spend a lot of time with many men." She took a bite of cake and chewed thoughtfully. "I keep telling myself it's time for me to change that, but I'm not sure."

"I would guess with children around, you have to be careful."

"Exactly." She leaned toward him. "Colton is young enough now that it's not an issue for you, but it will be as he gets older. I've been out with a few men, but so far I haven't met anyone I want to introduce to the boys. Although there is a nice sales rep where I work." She shrugged. "We'll have to see."

He glanced at the far end of the table and saw that Betsy's children were still occupied with their own conversation. "How did you manage to raise Cynthia on your own? You were so young."

"In a way that helped," she said. "I was too inexperienced to realize what a huge job I was taking on. So I was able to be confident and fearless, even when I didn't know what I was doing."

"You have tremendous character that you've passed onto your daughter. I admire that."

"Mine or hers?" she asked, then shook her head. "You don't have to answer that." She looked at her daughter. "Cynthia was there for me when I was going through a bad time. I'll never forget that, nor will her brothers and sister. She's a very special young woman. But being at home with me these past three years has meant that she couldn't have much of a social life of her own. She hasn't had the usual experiences other women her age have had."

As far as warnings went, it wasn't a very subtle one.

"I understand that you have concerns," he said stiffly. "I have no intention of hurting her."

Betsy stared at him. "Unfortunately it's not just your decision. I'll be honest. I've tried to warn her off you, but I don't think she's going to listen. Sometimes lessons have to be learned through personal experience. If you break her heart, she'll have to figure out a way to get over it."

Her pragmatic attitude surprised him. "Aren't you going to threaten me in some way if I break her heart?"

"No. I suspect that if you hurt my daughter, you'll punish yourself far more harshly and effectively than I ever could. Besides, I can't help wondering if you're the one meant to learn a lesson from all this rather than Cynthia. Wouldn't that be interesting?"

Sunday morning Jonathan sat in the dining room, reading the paper. Betsy and her children had left about ten the previous evening, after watching a movie in the media room. Surprisingly he'd enjoyed having them over for the evening and he'd been sorry to see them go.

"Have you recovered from the invasion?"

He looked up and saw Cynthia standing in the doorway of the dining room, holding Colton in her arms. She wore a long-sleeved robe that came to her ankles and her hair was loose.

In her shapeless outfit, clutching an infant, she was nothing like the women who usually made up his world. He could easily provide a list of all the things they didn't have in common and all the reasons a relationship with her wouldn't work. But that didn't stop the heat from slamming into him as he stared at her with hungry appreciation.

"I was just thinking that I enjoyed last night," he said, knowing that she was unlikely to read the need in his eyes. At times her innocence was a blessing. It kept her from figuring out what he was thinking, and acted as a reason for him to keep his distance.

"And now you can tell Brett and Brad apart." She smiled. "Very few people have figured that out."

Brett did most of the talking for the twins, but Brad was the quiet rebel. He had a small scar by his left eyebrow. The result of a close encounter with a coffee table when he'd been a toddler and both boys had been jumping on the sofa.

"Today is Lucinda's day off," she began.

"I'm aware of that."

"Good."

She walked forward and handed him Colton. The action was so unexpected that he found himself taking the baby and holding him awkwardly against his chest.

"I want to take a shower," she announced. "So you need to watch Colton for me until I'm done. I'll be back in about twenty minutes."

He stiffened and held the baby out at arm's length in front of him. "I can't do that. What if he needs something?"

Colton began to fuss, which made Jonathan sweat.

"Don't hold him like that," Cynthia said, reaching over and drawing the baby close to his chest. "Cuddle him. Pretend he's that big stuffed bear you brought me in the hospital."

"Not likely. I don't think you'd appreciate me leaving him propped up in the closet."

She pressed her lips together. "You know exactly what I mean. Now he's been fed and changed, so he's not going to need anything specific in the next half hour. Just get to know him."

She gave him a quick wave of her fingers, and then she was gone.

Jonathan stared down at the small child he held. Blue eyes so much like his own stared back at him.

"Now what?" he asked.

Colton didn't answer. Instead he waved a plump hand in the air and made a cooing sound.

"I don't suppose you're going to let me read the paper, are you?" he asked conversationally.

Colton surprised him by smiling. Involuntarily Jonathan smiled back, then shifted the baby so that he nestled in the crook of his left arm. The placement felt awkward, but it mimicked what he'd seen Cynthia do dozens of times. Colton didn't have high standards for his caretaker because he quickly relaxed and began a private baby game that required him to catch sight of his fingers, then waggle them in the air.

Jonathan looked at the boy. This living being was a part of his brother, David. David who had stolen from him and wanted him dead. Yet he wasn't angry at Colton. He wasn't anything at him. His lack of desire to be with the child was more about not knowing how to handle the situation than any avoidance based on emotion.

"Cynthia thinks it's important that we bond," he said.

Colton glanced up with interest.

"I thought we could wait until you're older. You know, when you have something to say."

Colton offered a gummy grin.

Jonathan knew that this infant was completely dependent. Without aid from the outside world, he would die in a matter of days. He, Jonathan, had once been this small and helpless. Smiling back at the baby he knew that he could never let anything happen to Colton. It wasn't because of blood ties or any feelings, but because it would be wrong. He might be fifteen kinds of a bastard, but he wasn't about to abandon his nephew.

Yet his father had turned his back on him. Without a second thought, the elder Steele had made Jonathan unwelcome in his own home. Not once, not even at the time of his death, had Jonathan's father once recanted his position.

"I won't do that to you," he said quietly, gently touching the boy's soft cheek. "I can't promise to love you because love is a dangerous thing to feel. But I won't make you unwelcome."

As the baby seemed to like the sound of his voice, Jonathan picked up the business section he'd been perusing and began to read aloud.

Some time later Cynthia walked back into the dining

room. She'd showered and changed into jeans and a shirt. The green-and-black plaid brought out the green in her eyes. Her hair hung loose around her face and a light touch of makeup accentuated her pretty features. The scent of fresh shampoo and soap teased him.

"It's Sunday," she announced, helping herself to coffee from the carafe in the center of the table. "I thought you might like to spend some time with Colton. Sort of a family thing. Although if you want me around to help with him, I'm happy to tag along."

He had a sudden vision of the three of them on a picnic, like a scene out of a TV movie. Or maybe they could just spend the day quietly at home.

Cynthia sat across from him and smiled. As she picked up her cup of coffee, her shirt tightened slightly, outlining her breasts. The need to pull her close and kiss her nearly overwhelmed him. He wanted her more than he'd ever wanted a woman before. Even though she was off limits and completely wrong for him. Or maybe those were the reasons why she appealed. Because she was different. Because with her at least one of them could possibly give a damn about what was happening.

The realization that he might want Cynthia to care about him drove him to his feet. He lived alone. That was how he preferred it. No one got in the way; no one got close.

He thrust Colton at her across the table. "I'm not interested in playing house with you," he said cruelly. "I want you to do your job, nothing more."

He walked out of the dining room, then out of the house. He decided to go to work because he couldn't think of anywhere else to go.

But once at the office, he found he couldn't concentrate. For the first time in his life, he couldn't get lost in spreadsheets and projections. The words and numbers were meaningless. All he could see was the hurt in Cynthia's eyes and the way she'd flinched from his words.

"I warned her," he muttered to himself, but the phrase didn't help. Nor did telling himself she would get over it.

He'd never allowed himself to play with anyone out of his league. He was careful to choose companions who understood, women like Martha Jean Porter. Slick, experienced and as coldly calculating as himself. His date with her was in less than a week. At least then he could take care of the ache that filled him. It was just an itch, he told himself, and she was the exact woman to scratch it.

Cynthia brushed away the tears on her cheeks and told herself she was a fool for crying over Jonathan Steele. "He's your client, nothing else," she reminded herself. They didn't have a personal relationship.

But it had felt personal when he'd kissed her and again last night when he'd laughed and joked with her family. It had felt good and right and she'd allowed herself to make-believe that all this was real.

"But it's not, is it?" she asked softly.

Colton gurgled, then reached for a loose strand of hair. She eased the lock from the baby's grip and tried not to give in to more tears. "You're not mine," she said, holding the sweet-smelling baby close. "This is work and I mustn't let myself care about you too much. Jonathan is going to get a permanent nanny and then I'll be gone."

But as she held the now-familiar weight of the happy child, she had a bad feeling that it was too late for this lecture to help much. Since moving into Jonathan's house she'd been so caught up by the man himself, so concerned about the temptation to get close that she hadn't thought to keep her heart safe from either him or his nephew. Now she was in danger of falling in love with both of them. To be honest, she didn't know who it would be harder to leave.

The smart thing would be to walk away. She had several nannies working for her and any one of them would be a qualified replacement. Except her mother hadn't raised her to be a quitter.

*I'm not interested in playing house.*

Jonathan's words cut through her like a knife. She replayed them again and again in her mind wondering how he'd known that's what she was doing. Pretending that she really belonged here, that he cared about her and that Colton was the baby they would raise together. A foolish dream.

Humiliation washed over her and with it a resolve that she wouldn't act that way again. She wasn't going to let him catch her daydreaming again. She would do what was expected and nothing more. When the time was up, she would walk away with her head held high.

As for her heart and its attachment to both of the Steele men…there was nothing she could do about that now. The damage was done. When she was gone she would have plenty of time to figure out how to put her life back together.

## Chapter 9

Jack Stryker cradled his cup of coffee as he sat in one of the leather chairs on the opposite side of Jonathan's desk.

"The FBI is being closedmouthed about what they're doing," Stryker was saying. "The fact that they're involved means David was dealing with some interesting people."

"Any news about the two cars that went tearing out of the hotel parking lot that night?"

"Nothing concrete. The first guy—probably the shooter—got away. The second guy crashed. He's pretty beat-up and doesn't remember who he is."

Jonathan considered the information. Was the second man an accomplice or law enforcement? Obviously Stryker didn't know either.

"So they don't know who shot David and Lisa?"

Stryker shrugged. "If they've figured it out, they're not telling me. They've expanded the scope of their investigation, which means the illegal activities reaches past Grand Springs." He took a sip of coffee. "Not a big surprise there."

Jonathan tried to imagine how David had gotten involved with people who would eventually kill him.

"The good news is you're going to get your money back," Stryker said. "At least all that we can find. The rough estimate is about eighty percent."

It took Jonathan a couple of seconds to figure out what the other man was talking about. "The money David embezzled?"

The detective nodded. "He hadn't taken that out in cash. Instead it was put in several of his accounts. We've got our police accountants tracing it right now. Like I said, we're guessing we're going to recover most of it."

"Great," Jonathan said, trying to get excited. But the truth was, the money wasn't all that important to him. He didn't need it to keep the company running. What he wanted was answers. Who had killed his brother and sister-in-law and why?

Stryker set his coffee cup on the edge of Jonathan's desk. "That about does it for me, unless you have any other questions."

"None that you can answer."

The two men rose and shook hands, then Jonathan walked the detective to the door.

"We'll be in touch," Stryker told him.

When he was alone again, Jonathan walked to the expanse of window behind his desk. From his high-rise office, he had a view of downtown Grand Springs, such as it was. The town wasn't very big and more than once he'd considered moving the corporate headquarters to a larger city. But he never had. To him, this was home.

But thinking about home was a mistake. It made him remember his conversation with Cynthia the previous day, when he'd told her he wasn't interested in playing house and had walked out angry. Although he'd been back, he hadn't seen her last evening. Mostly because he'd stayed in his office, not sure what he was supposed to say.

He knew that his words had hurt her—something he'd wanted to avoid if possible. But she was so damn innocent and he couldn't figure out what she wanted from him. Whatever it was, he had a reasonable suspicion that he was going to fail at delivering it. She thought he was some kind of saint while he knew the truth. He was a sorry excuse for a man and he didn't have a prayer of being even half of what she expected.

He told himself it didn't matter. That her good opinion was meaningless. He told himself that she would be out of his life in a matter of weeks, and then he would never have to see her again. That wanting her was simply a physical reaction to a long period of celibacy and that once he did the wild thing with Martha Jean this weekend, all the aching would fade.

But it wasn't just about sex, he realized, even though he didn't want to admit it to himself. Cynthia intrigued him on multiple levels. Her innate ability to see the best in people, despite evidence to the contrary. Her affection and ease with Colton. Her fearlessness. She stood up to him, saying things no one had ever dared. It was as if she believed her convictions would keep her safe.

Without knowing why he was doing it or what he hoped to accomplish, Jonathan left his office. His stunned secretary stood in the hallway reading from his busy schedule.

"Cancel all my meetings for the rest of the day," he told her as the elevator doors closed behind him.

Thirty minutes later he walked into his house and upstairs to the baby's room. He found Cynthia and Colton sitting on a blanket in a patch of sunshine. There were piles of brightly colored plastic blocks around them. Colton was on his stomach, raised up on his arms. He smiled when he saw Jonathan.

Cynthia looked up. "We were discussing dinner," she said lightly. "It's about time to start introducing him to solid foods. We've spent a bit of the last four days getting used to sitting in a high chair. I suggested a menu of rice cereal but Colton is leaning toward a fruit or vegetable baby food. You want to cast the deciding vote?"

The words sounded fine, but he saw the hint of pain still lurking in her eyes.

He looked around the room. What once had been a generic guest room was now baby paradise. Lucinda had arranged for a border print of teddy bears in a marching band. She'd told him that she would pick out something with cars when Colton got older. Soft, pastel stuffed animals sat on a shelf across from the window. There was a crib in the center of the room, a changing table against a wall. A child lived here. A child who was his responsibility. How the hell had that happened?

He turned to Cynthia who still sat on the floor. She wore her usual uniform of jeans and a sweatshirt, while Colton had on a bright blue one-piece romper.

"What do you want from me?" he asked, then motioned to the room. "Isn't providing this enough?"

"*I* don't want anything," she said. "This isn't about me, it's about Colton."

She was both lying and telling the truth, he thought.

They had two issues with each other. Their relationship, if that's what anyone would call it, and his nephew. Jonathan decided it would be a whole lot easier to talk about the latter.

"I've taken care of Colton," he said. "He has a home, someone to see to his needs."

"You have a responsibility to do more than pay the bills," she said, scrambling to her feet.

She'd pulled her long blond hair back into a ponytail and hadn't bothered with any makeup. She looked young and impossibly out of her league, yet she didn't act intimidated or afraid. Instead she moved closer to him.

"Colton is family," she said. "Your family. From what I can tell, he's the only family you have left. But do you respect that or act like it matters? No. You ignore him."

"He's a baby. We're hardly going to have a meaningful discussion about world peace."

"Agreed. But that's no reason not to develop a relationship with him."

He waved a hand at her. "I'm not interested in this."

"So what?" She moved closer and placed her hands on her hips. "We all have to do things that might not be our first choice. It's called being an adult and dealing with our responsibilities. Right now Colton is one of your responsibilities. This isn't about business or some annoying social obligation. We're discussing the life of a child. How dare you dismiss the importance of that?"

Anger flared in her hazel-green eyes. Her breath came in sharp gasps as if she hung onto her control by a thread.

"Quit being so damn selfish," she said, poking his chest with her finger. "Yes, you had a lousy relationship with your own father. Yes, your brother was the favorite. So what? Get over it. You have a wonderful life now. One of your own making. You have many accomplishments that have brought you prestige and great wealth. But none of those matter. If you don't get your act together you're going to do to Colton exactly what your father did to you.''

Her words slammed into him, ripping through his façade of calm civility and anchoring in still-open wounds. He didn't want to be like his father.

But that wasn't what he was doing, he told himself. It couldn't be. He might not care about Colton, but he didn't actively dislike the child. His feelings were more neutral. He made sure that Colton had everything he could need.

As his father had done with him, a small voice whispered in his head.

Cynthia seemed to sense the battle being waged within him. But rather than backing off, she moved in for the kill. ''What kind of legacy are you going to leave, Jonathan Steele? A hundred years from now you'll be dead. Will anyone at Steele Enterprises remember the man you were? I don't think so. But Colton's children will know. What do you want your nephew to say about you? That you were a great man, stern and honest, yet always available and filled with a giving heart? Or that you were a distant relative who gave him up to the hired help to raise?''

Her words rang in the silence. He tried to think of something to say to dispute them, but what was there? Everything she said was true.

He took a step back, then turned away. He didn't want to be like his father, but he wasn't sure he could change.

"You're better than this," she said softly. "This isn't who you are."

He gave a sharp laugh. "It's exactly who I am. I warned you."

"Then it's time to change and be someone else."


Jonathan did his best to ignore everything Cynthia had told him. He and his father had little in common—he wasn't treating Colton the same way he'd been treated. But there was too much truth for him to avoid it. He had many flaws, but self-delusion wasn't one of them.

In between meetings and while in the car over the next three days, he replayed parts of their conversation. What *would* Colton think about him as he grew up? Jonathan knew that he would never forget or forgive his own father's inattention, the way the elder Steele had made Jonathan feel like an interloper in his own home. He was going to have to change the present or he was destined to repeat the past. But how?

With no obvious answer to the question, he made his way from the garage to the house. He hadn't seen Cynthia or Colton since Monday, three days ago. But tonight he'd come home earlier than usual with the thought that he might talk to her. Not that he knew what he was going to say.

He opened the front door and was immediately assaulted by loud music. Not rock, but something with the distinct rhythm of a waltz. In front of him Lucinda moved down the stairs.

"The baby, he sleeps through all of this," she said loudly as she approached and took his briefcase. "It's Miss Cynthia. She's teaching her sister how to dance." A maternal smile softened Lucinda's face. "There is a school dance this weekend. Something about ballroom dancing.'' She jerked her head toward the living room. "They're in there.''

Jonathan loosened his tie. He walked into the living room and stood just inside the doorway. The sofas and occasional tables had been pushed up against the wall, while the rug covering the hardwood floors had been rolled out of the way.

Cynthia and Jenny stood in the center of the open space, facing each other. As he watched, Cynthia assumed the position of the man and put her hand on her sister's waist. They were both in jeans and sweatshirts, but Jenny had slipped on a pair of high heels. Now she glanced down at her shoes.

"I hate these,'' she complained. "I keep feeling like I'm going to tip over.''

"I know, but you're wearing them with your dress so you need to get used to them.''

Cynthia wore athletic shoes, so she was only a couple of inches taller than her sister. Both females had pulled their hair back into ponytails. Viewed from the side, he could see the similarities in their profiles and posture. Jenny was still a young girl but in time she would be as lovely as her sister.

"Remember,'' Cynthia was saying. "Listen to the music. A waltz has a very specific beat. If you can begin to feel it as well as hear it, you'll find it easier to dance. One, two, three, one, two, three.''

As she spoke, music from a portable CD player blared into the room. It covered the sound of Jonathan's steps and he was able to step farther into the room, then lean up against the wall.

The sisters moved well together. Jenny hesitated a few times, but obviously had the general idea down. It was just a matter of practice. Cynthia patiently led her through the movements again and again.

He studied the woman who had invaded his life and demanded much from him. Not for herself but for a baby she'd known only a couple of weeks. What would she be like if she were defending an offspring of her own?

He knew instinctively that Cynthia would protect her baby with a fierceness that rivaled any in nature. She would never abandon her child, walking away without a second glance. For the early and formative years of her life she'd been raised by a single mother who had faced incredible odds to keep her small family together. To Cynthia there was no greater bond than that of blood kin.

They couldn't be more opposite. He still believed that families were nothing but pain and trouble. Look at what his own brother had done to him. Yet even know-ing what she did about him, Cynthia still expected him to open his life and his heart to his nephew. She ex-pected him to have the same giving nature as herself.

He wanted to dismiss her as foolish and innocent, but a part of him wondered if she might not be the stronger of the two of them. Didn't her capacity to love and forgive mean that her emotional boundaries were greater?

For reasons that were not clear to him, she saw the best in him. She had unreasonable expectations of his nature and personality. Even when he tried to convince her that he wasn't anything she imagined, she persisted in assuming the best. Her attitude was so different from any he'd ever experienced. She was a fool and yet in some small back corner of his being he was pleased and flattered by her opinion, however false and undeserved.

Now, as she danced with her sister, she caught sight of him. Instead of a welcoming smile, she gave him a tentative nod. Questions flickered in her eyes and there was a tremor at the corner of her mouth. He hated that he'd damaged her ability to believe in him. Which only went to show how perverse human nature could be. After working to convince her he was a bastard, now he was disappointed he'd finally gotten her to believe the truth. He hated that he missed her open and honest admiration, even if it was based on a fairy tale.

"How about the male perspective on this whole thing?" he asked, walking toward the two women.

Jenny looked up and saw him, then blushed. When she ducked her head she looked so much like her sister. A younger version, just as innocent, just as willing to lead with her heart.

"Mr. Steele," Jenny said and stepped away from her sister. "I'm horrible at this. Cynthia is trying to help me, but I don't guess I'm ever going to get it."

"I think you're doing very well." He stepped in front of her and held out his arms. "May I have this dance?" he asked as the CD quieted for a couple of seconds before moving to the next selection.

"I, um…" Jenny glanced at her sister who nodded encouragingly, then smiled shyly at Jonathan. "Okay. I'll try not to step on your toes."

"I'll do the same."

His comment earned him a quick laugh, then she sobered as she mouthed the one-two-three count of the waltz.

Jonathan waited until she was on "one" then began to move. He took small steps, using their joined hands to give her a sense of the direction they would go next.

Jenny stumbled twice, then seemed to catch on to the dance.

They waltzed around the room together, developing a rhythm that nearly matched that of the music. Her young face screwed up with concentration as she focused on staying in step.

As they turned, he caught sight of Cynthia. Some of her tentativeness had fled. Warmth and gratitude took its place. He realized that by taking the time to dance with her sister, he'd found his way back into Cynthia's good graces. He wanted to be cynical and remind her that he was far from a nice guy, but he found himself pleased by *her* pleasure.

"Don't look at your feet," Cynthia called.

Jenny jerked up her head, then stumbled and would have fallen if he hadn't caught her. She mumbled an embarrassed apology.

"Don't worry about it," Jonathan said. "How about if you watch for a few minutes and catch your breath?"

"I'd like that," the teenager said.

He turned to Cynthia and held out his hands. "Care to provide a demonstration?"

Cynthia walked over to stand in front of him. She wore jeans and a sweatshirt, not a ball gown. Whatever makeup she'd put on in the morning had faded and her hair was slipping free of its ponytail. Even so, he thought she was as lovely as she'd been the first night they'd met.

He took her in his arms and they began to dance.

They moved easily together, swaying and turning in time with the music. While he'd held Jenny at arm's length, he drew Cynthia up against him so they were nearly touching. He could feel the heat of her body. Her breasts were close enough to tease him and he longed to have their interested audience gone so that he could lean down and kiss her.

"The key is to relax," Cynthia called to her sister. "Let the man pick the direction. Shift your weight after each step and you'll be able to pivot in any direction."

The lesson continued for nearly an hour, with Jenny dancing with Jonathan again. This time she was able to look at him almost as much as she looked at her feet.

"Excellent," Cynthia said when the CD ended. "You're going to be wonderful tomorrow night."

"I hope so," Jenny said doubtfully. "At least the boys won't be any better than me." She bit her lower lip. "What if none of them want to dance with me?"

"They will," Jonathan said. "You're going to be the prettiest girl there, which is both good and bad. Pretty girls can be scary. But you're also funny and nice, which makes guys feel comfortable. I think your big problem is going to be deciding who you want to dance with."

Jenny blushed again, but this time from pleasure. "You really think so?"

"I know so."

She laughed, then hugged Cynthia close. "I hope Jonathan is right."

"I'll bet he is," her sister told her.

Lucinda walked into the living room. She'd pulled on a coat over her uniform. "Mr. Jonathan, I put dinner in the refrigerator. It needs forty minutes at 350." She winked at Cynthia. "I don't know why I'm telling him. As if he's going to be the one to heat up the food." She looked at Jenny. "Are you ready to go?"

"Yes." Jenny slipped off her high heels, then walked over to her backpack. She put on the loafers waiting there then shrugged into her jacket and tucked her pumps into a shoebox.

"Are you sure about taking Jenny home?" Cynthia asked. "I can do it."

"No." Lucinda dismissed her with a wave. "I'm going to an early show at the movies and your house is right on my way. Come on, little one. I'll give you advice about boys on the way over."

They said their goodbyes and left. When Jonathan and Cynthia were alone, they both shifted awkwardly in the suddenly quiet room.

"I'm sorry about what I said the other day," she said quickly while avoiding his gaze. "I was judging you and that's wrong. Despite your lack of relationship with your brother, you must still be in shock over his death. It's going to take time to come to terms with that. You've also had to get used to the idea of being a father. Most men have about nine months to absorb that information, but you've had less than a month. It makes sense that you need more time."

He stared at her. She seemed fascinated by the CD player, studying it with an intensity of a scientist viewing a new form of life.

"How can you make excuses for me?" he asked. "I was cruel to you."

"You were in shock."

"I was out of line and I'm sorry." Like a wounded animal, he'd lashed out. For as long as he lived he would never forget her stricken expression when he'd told her he wasn't interested in playing house. "You were right about a lot of things you said a few days ago. About Colton." He hesitated. "I don't know what I'm going to do about him, but I don't want to repeat my father's mistakes."

She finally looked up at him and smiled. "I'm glad."

Her hazel-green eyes glowed with adoration. It was something he didn't want to see there because it made it too easy for him to imagine how amicable she would be to almost any suggestions. And since meeting her, he'd had several in mind.

"Dance with me," he said before he could stop himself.

Instead of answering, she pushed a button on the CD player, then adjusted a knob. Soft music filled the room. She moved toward him and he took her in his arms.

She felt so right next to him, he thought, wishing she were older and more experienced. If she were more in his league he wouldn't have to feel so guilty about his desire. Yet if she was different, he wasn't sure he would want her as much.

But the scent of her intoxicated him and made him want more. He rubbed his thumb against her palm as they danced. She shuddered.

"Hell," he muttered, then abandoned the waltz and drew her close. They were barely moving in the center of the living room. Her breasts pressed into his chest, burning him, making him ache. His arousal was as instant as it was hard. Her stomach barely touched him there and he wanted to press against her—as if that would ease his need.

"Talk about something," he commanded, desperate for a distraction.

"What?" Her voice sounded dreamy. "Oh. Okay. Well, Colton had a doctor's appointment today. It was just a well-baby checkup. Fortunately he's been healthy since birth. He's right where he should be as far as height, weight and development. The doctor agreed with me on starting him on solid food pretty soon."

He looked down at her upraised face. "You mentioned that before."

She nodded. "Switching over is necessary, but the baby has to be ready to make the change. If we begin too early, it will be a fight and we're potentially setting up years of battling over food. If we start too late, he could be fussy about what kind of foods he enjoys." She smiled. "Even if it goes well, I have to warn you that it's a very messy proposition."

We. She kept saying we, as if he had a part in all this. "I know I have to make some changes to include Colton in my life," he said. "I'm not sure what they're going to be."

"You don't have to decide today. He's not going anywhere. Just don't take too long."

Forgiveness glowed in her eyes. Forgiveness and something he wanted to believe was desire.

"Don't be so softhearted where I'm concerned," he said gruffly. "You're letting me off the hook too easily."

"I can't help what I feel," she said.

He wanted to say the same thing, but couldn't. This wasn't right, he told himself, even as he wanted to find a way to make it, if not correct, then possible.

"I'm not worth it," he said.

"You are to me."

She stared up at him as if he had the power to light up the sky. Her words told him everything—that she was his for the taking. He knew he was the biggest bastard alive, but he wasn't ready to cross that line yet. Not with someone so close to innocent.

He came to a stop in the center of the room, then cupped her face in his hands. "All I want to do is take you upstairs and make love with you," he admitted. "You have to tell me no."

"Why?"

The single word cut him down to his soul. He sucked in a breath. "Because you haven't been with many men and I'm more than capable of seducing you."

She smiled. A sweet, feminine smile that spoke of the power of surrender. "Who says you'd have to try?"

He told himself to fight her acquiescence. He told himself to be a better man than he wanted and walk away. He told himself he wouldn't be able to face himself in the mirror if he did this. Then he realized he didn't care about any of that. He wanted her more than he'd ever wanted anyone before.

He swore under his breath and swung her up in his arms. She gave a soft cry of surprise, then snuggled against him. As he carried her out of the room, she reached out and snagged the baby monitor resting on a table, then wrapped her arms around him.

"Don't worry," she whispered in his ear. "I trust you."

"That," he told her, "is the problem."

# Chapter 10

This was the perfect conclusion to the fairy tale that had started in her rented Cinderella gown, Cynthia thought dreamily as Jonathan carried her upstairs. The handsome prince had, if not fallen in love with her, certainly begun to care. Now, overwhelmed by passion, he wanted to make love with her.

Thousands of thoughts floated through her brain, but she couldn't catch on to any one of them. Which was fine. She just wanted to close her eyes and get lost in the wonder of being held in Jonathan's strong arms. He was everything she'd ever wanted in a man. Not only was he intelligent and capable, but he didn't always insist on being right. After she'd explained the problem with Colton and how he had to start to bond with the boy, Jonathan had actually listened. While it would be difficult for him, he was going to let go of the past enough to let his nephew into his life.

"What are you thinking?" Jonathan asked as he stopped and let her slide to her feet.

She opened her eyes and looked around. They were in his bedroom. At least she assumed it was his—she'd never actually been inside this room before. But if the huge four-poster bed and slightly masculine furnishings were anything to go by, this was where Jonathan slept.

Her gaze wandered around the room, then returned to the bed. As she took in the dimensions of the mattress, a few drops of reality trickled down her spine. Bed...mattress...as in sex? She swallowed.

"Cynthia?"

"What? Oh, you wanted to know what I was thinking. Right." Except she couldn't remember. She took a step back and clutched the baby monitor to her chest. "Colton was up all morning with the doctor's visit. He seemed to really enjoy himself there. All the activity, I guess. Anyway, he'll probably sleep a little longer than usual this afternoon. Maybe for another hour or so."

She blinked several times as she stared at Jonathan and hoped she didn't look as stupid as she felt. Were they going to do it? Not that she didn't want to. While they'd been dancing together she'd felt all warm and melty inside. But dancing was very different from "the act."

"You're scared," he said flatly.

"Scared is a little too strong. I'm nervous." More nervous than she was willing to let on. Jonathan had hinted that he knew she was inexperienced, which was true, but she doubted he had a clue about *how* inexperienced. She glanced over her shoulder and saw that he'd closed the door behind them. It was very private. They were completely alone. Was that a good thing?

He smiled. "Do you remember me telling you that I

was as dangerous as a wolf and that I could hurt you? You stood up to me, saying that would never happen. Have you changed your mind?''

She swallowed again. ''Not exactly. It's just this is, well, different.''

''Do you want to leave? I won't pressure you to stay. It's your decision.''

She hated that. Couldn't he just seduce her? Except Jonathan was too good a man for that. He wouldn't kiss her and touch her, making her so weak and aroused that she no longer had possession of her senses. Instead he forced her to act like an adult and accept the consequences of her actions.

Resolutely she walked over to the nightstand and put down the baby monitor. She adjusted the volume button, then turned to face him. ''I want this,'' she said, her voice shaking only a little.

He smiled and crossed the floor to stand in front of her. ''I'm guessing you haven't been with a man like me before,'' he said. ''By that I mean someone older and a lot more experienced.''

''Right on the first try.'' She was trying for sophisticated but had the bad feeling that she sounded breathy and nervous instead.

''I promise to go slowly. If you don't like something I'm doing or if you want me to do it differently, just tell me. I want this to be good for you.''

''Okay.''

What she wanted was for it to be over, she thought, but doubted he would want to hear that. Jonathan reached for her. There was a split second of hesitation on his part, as if he was giving her one last chance to change her mind. Cynthia quickly searched her heart and mind. Was this what she wanted? She'd waited twenty-six years before making love with a man. Was this the right time for her?

Then his arms were around her and he was drawing her close to him. As she moved into his embrace and the now familiar warmth of his body surrounded her, she had the sensation of coming home. As if being with this man was her one best and true destiny. She didn't want anyone else to touch her or kiss her. Only Jonathan. Not just because he was so handsome, but because he was so good on the inside. Because all her life she'd been waiting for someone to feel as right to her as Frank had felt to her mother. And Jonathan was that man.

He brushed her mouth with his. The searing heat surprised her and forced her up onto her toes. She pressed against him so they were touching from shoulder to knee. She needed to be close. She needed to feel her breasts flatten against his chest and his lips exploring hers. She angled her head and parted her mouth, wanting him inside of her.

His hands splayed against her back. She clung to his shoulders. His tongue brushed against the inside of her lower lip, then dipped into her mouth. When he stroked her she gasped and opened wider, needing the contact.

The touch of his tongue was as magical as she remembered. The heat increased until she thought she might be on fire. She could feel flames of desire licking along her arms and legs. Warmth pooled in her breasts, and lower, in her belly.

Conscious thought seemed to flee her brain. She couldn't think in sentences, only in pictures and impressions. He still wore his suit jacket and she suddenly needed that layer of clothing gone. She slipped her hands under the lapels and pushed it down his arms. He released her long enough to shrug out of the garment.

Then his hands returned to her body, but this time they weren't still. He stroked her back, moving up and down until he cupped her rear and pulled her against him. She arched into him, her belly flat against him. Her attention focused on that most male part of him. She wanted to know if he was aroused...as he had been the last time.

Pleasure shot through her as she felt a hard ridge nestling against her stomach. He rubbed back and forth, then groaned. As if touching her excited him. Her! She was barely knowledgeable enough to know how to kiss, yet she'd managed to turn him on.

He placed his hands on her waist and urged her forward. She felt him bump into the bed, then he settled onto the mattress and pulled her into the vee of his open legs. She went willingly. His hands moved from her waist to the hem of her sweatshirt. There was a slight tug.

She opened her eyes. Jonathan sat at eye level. Even as she watched him watch her, he drew her shirt up and over her head. Her throat went dry and she had to fight to keep from raising her hands to cover herself. Although she'd had boyfriends before, things had never really progressed much past kissing. Any contact with her breasts had been made through layers of clothing. Certainly no one had been bold enough to simply start undressing her.

Still, some of her nervousness eased when Jonathan stared at her peach lace bra and swallowed. "You've got something against plain white cotton?" he asked.

She frowned. "Is that what you prefer?"

"Not at all, but at least then I might have a chance at controlling myself. Although with you, I have my doubts." He leaned forward and placed a kiss on the exposed skin of her left breast. "So very pretty," he murmured.

She'd never thought of her body as anything but functional. Did he really think she was pretty? But before she could ask, he reached behind her and expertly unfastened her bra. No tugging, no fumbling. In fact that man did it better than she did.

And then the scrap of lace and straps was gone and the cool late-afternoon air moved against her breasts. *He could see her,* she thought in amazement, then clamped her eyes shut. He might be able to see her, but she certainly did not want to see him.

"Kiss me," he murmured, drawing her against him again.

She did as he requested, trying not to think about her bare breasts. But for the moment he seemed to be ignoring them in favor of her back. His strong, warm hands moved up and down her bare skin. The contact made her shiver, but in a good way. He traced her spine, then slipped around her waistband and up her ribs.

She couldn't think about the kiss anymore. She could only focus on the feel on his hands moving higher and higher. She stopped breathing. What was it going to feel like? Would she like it when he touched her there. She froze, her lips a scant inch from his. Then his fingers found her curves and he stroked her tight nipples.

A hot, electric shiver raced through her. Every cell in her body turned its attention to her puckered, sensitive nipples that had suddenly become the center of her being. He stroked and teased so lightly, yet everything he did was wonderful.

She continued not to breathe, but now from pleasure rather than panic. She was terrified that if she moved in any way, he would stop.

"Do you like that?" he asked.

She risked opening her eyes and saw that he was looking at her. Without thinking, she glanced down and saw his tanned fingers moving against her pale breasts. Instantly a hot blush flared and she made to cover herself.

"Don't," he said softly. "I was wrong. You're more than pretty, you're beautiful. I want to look and touch and make you feel everything possible. I want you as hungry for me as I am for you." He cupped her curves and used his thumbs to continue to tease her nipples. "Do you like it?" he asked again.

"Yes," she forced out, barely able to speak for all the sensations washing through her. "A lot."

He chuckled, then ducked his head. Before she knew what he was going to do, he leaned forward and drew her nipple into his mouth. His lips closed around her and he sucked very gently.

Cynthia felt her mouth drop open. She'd read about this of course, but reading and experiencing had little in common. She always thought the idea of a man doing something like that was a little silly and...

His tongue circled her, then flicked over the tight peak. She breathed his name and decided that she really needed to expand her horizons and keep trying new things. This wasn't silly at all. It was wonderful.

She felt as if her core temperature had increased about ten degrees. Her thighs trembled. Between her legs was a dampness she couldn't remember having many times before, along with a persistent ache she'd noticed earlier. She felt sort of squirmy and tense, but also languid in a way that made her unconcerned when he moved to her other breast and suckled that nipple.

Slowly she brought her hands up to cup his face. She

felt the faint rasp of stubble and the crisp cool ends of his dark hair. She explored the shape of his ears and the feel of the skin at the back of his neck.

When he pushed her away, her first thought was that he'd changed his mind. But before she could panic, he'd dropped to one knee and was unfastening her shoes. When she stepped out of them, he pulled off her socks, then returned to the bed.

His fingers sought the button at the waistband of her jeans. It unfastened as easily as her bra. Next he lowered her zipper. Large, masculine hands pushed down her jeans and panties in one, smooth movement. The next thing she knew, she was standing completely naked in front of him.

There wasn't time to be nervous, though. Before the first panicky thought could form, she was back in his arms and he was kissing her. He urged her to straddle his thighs and she went willingly, settling her weight on him. The position left her feeling a little vulnerable, especially when one of his hands rested on her bare leg. But the kissing was so good and there was always the hope that he would touch her breasts again, so she really didn't mind...even as he began to move higher and higher.

Then he was so close to the apex of her thighs that she couldn't ignore it any longer. Keeping her eyes closed, she dropped her forehead to his shoulder. One hand rubbed up and down her back while the other crept between her blond curls and touched her most secret place.

She'd read about Sleeping Beauty being awakened by a single kiss, but she'd never heard about anyone being changed by a single touch. Until now. She didn't know if it was good luck on his part or design or what, but his fingers found one tiny spot that seemed to be magic.

At the first moment of contact, she nearly shot to her feet. Every muscle tensed, but only because the sensation was so incredibly wonderful. It was even better than when he'd touched her nipples. She gasped and clung to him, while he laughed softly.

"Got it in one," he murmured and began to kiss her neck.

"Yeah," she said, not sure what she was agreeing to, but also not caring.

He continued to touch her there. Gently, so very gently, but with a persistence that made her muscles quiver. She wanted him never to stop. It felt too good. She would have done anything, said anything, just to have him continue.

"I could never be a spy," she whispered. "If I had any secrets, you would only have to touch me like this to get me to tell them all."

"Do you have any secrets?" he asked teasingly.

"No. Do you want me to make any up?"

She didn't hear his answer. Mostly because she wasn't listening. She couldn't. Not while he continued to touch her there, moving back and forth on that one spot. Occasionally he drifted away, exploring the rest of her feminine place. Once he dipped his finger inside of her, as if testing the most private part of her.

Does it feel this good for the man, she wondered hazily as he returned to the tiny spot of pleasure and continued to take her on an odyssey of discovery. It had to, but at this point in time, she didn't really care. She just wanted to keep feeling the delightful tension that made her strain toward him. The fact that she was completely naked, on his lap, having him touch her so intimately was incidental.

Suddenly they were moving. Jonathan picked her up and turned her so she stretched out on the bed. He pulled off his shirt and tie, then his shoes and socks. Last to go were his slacks. He left on his briefs. Her gaze settled on the visible proof of his arousal. Two parts curiosity, one part fear made her shiver. Soon he was going to be inside of her.

"I want you," Jonathan breathed as he moved over her and began kissing her.

She wrapped her arms around him, drawing him close. As his tongue entered her mouth, his fingers returned to her waiting heat. He settled on that special spot and began to move faster.

Suddenly she couldn't breathe. Something was happening. The heat increased and her skin felt incredibly sensitive. Jonathan broke their kiss to move down to her breasts. He drew one nipple into his mouth and flicked it with his tongue. The rhythm matched his fingers below. The combination was indescribable. Involuntarily her knees drew back and her hips arched upward. He rubbed lighter and faster, over and over until she felt herself on the verge of either flying away or coming apart.

Then he was kissing her lips again. He dipped into her mouth and retreated. She followed. As she did, his lips closed around her and he gently sucked on her tongue. At the same movement, he increased the pressure between her legs. Tension grew unbearably.

Suddenly she was both flying and falling, caught up in a vortex, she neither understood nor wanted to leave. Every part of her body experienced a pleasure so complete she wondered how she'd survived without it for so long. His hands slowed, their kiss ended and she found herself cradled in his arms.

He didn't say anything, which was good because she felt a little embarrassed by what had happened. Had she said anything stupid or done it wrong?

"Thank you," Jonathan said, pressing a kiss to her forehead. "Not only for being so responsive, but for making it clear what you liked. I wanted to please you."

She risked a glance. He seemed genuinely happy so she smiled. "You did a really good job." The words were so inadequate that she had to laugh.

He grinned in return. "A good job, huh? Wow. Talk about praise. I'll have to get a plaque made."

Then they were laughing together and suddenly it was all right. Cynthia hugged Jonathan and he hugged her back.

"Thank you," she said. "I was really nervous and not sure how it was going to go. You made me feel wonderful."

"I'm glad."

Their gazes locked. She breathed his name and he kissed her. Slowly…deeply. Surprisingly her passion returned and with it the need to touch him and finally find out what all the fuss was about. She pressed her hands against his back and explored his powerful muscles. He was warm and smooth and felt so good to touch. He returned her caresses, first brushing her side, then teasing her breasts.

When her breathing had increased and she felt the now familiar heat flaring inside of her, he rolled away and opened a drawer on the nightstand. After pulling off his briefs, he removed the protection from its wrapping and slipped it on.

Cynthia rose up on her elbow to watch, but his back

was to her and she couldn't see very much. When he turned toward her, she caught only a brief glimpse of his maleness before he began kissing her again.

This time he knelt between her legs and cupped her face in his hands. His kisses were slow and drugging, leaving her aroused and panting. She felt something probing against her feminine place, then he was filling her.

"I want you," he breathed against her mouth, his dark gaze finding hers. "I'm not sure I can hold back."

Ah, cryptic conversation. "Me, either," she lied, hoping it was the right line.

Jonathan frowned. "I wouldn't think you'd have the same problem."

Not knowing how to respond, she wrapped her arms around his neck and kissed him thoroughly. That seemed to be enough of a distraction that he stopped talking.

She felt him continue to enter her. He was big and she stretched to the point of discomfort. Yet even as she wanted to protest, she had to admit she liked the feel of him inside of her. The fullness and pressure felt right, as if this was where he belonged.

He stopped for a second. "You're really tight." Then he pushed harder and there was a sharp pain.

She tensed, even as she realized what had happened. Goodbye to her virginity. There wasn't any fear or regret—only a sense of conviction that she'd made the correct choice. But Jonathan didn't seem to share her feelings. He'd stopped moving and when she opened her eyes, she found him staring at her.

"Tell me I'm wrong," he said, something close to panic filling his eyes.

The kissing had worked last time so she tried it again.

"I want you," she told him, echoing his words, then claiming his mouth. At the same time she placed her hands on his rear and pulled him in deeper.

He groaned as he buried himself inside of her. As he withdrew, he pulled back a little. "Are you sure?"

"Yes. Please. I want this."

He swore, then dropped his mouth to hers and claimed her. As his tongue invaded her mouth, the most male part of him invaded her in other ways. They moved together. The back and forth movement was interesting. She felt some of the same tinglings she'd felt earlier, but before she could decide on the possibilities, he was thrusting faster and deeper and she sensed that his time was near.

Then he cried out and stiffened. She held him close and smiled.

Jonathan rolled onto his back and stared unseeingly at the ceiling. His brain didn't want to process the facts, but he couldn't avoid them. Cynthia had been a virgin. A virgin! He hadn't known there were any left. At least not in her age bracket.

"You said you were twenty-six," he said, his voice accusing.

"I am."

"But..."

He turned to face her. She was naked and looking a little lost. Damn. Just like a kicked kitten. He didn't need this trouble in his life and he had exactly no one else to blame. He shifted and held out his arms so that she could cuddle against him. She sighed and a warm puff of air caressed his chest.

"How did this happen?" he asked. "The virgin part."

"Actually, I was born this way," she teased.

"Great." He took a deep breath and told himself to remain calm. Taking her virginity wasn't the end of the world…even if it felt that way. "I was more interested in how you stayed one."

"Oh." She tilted her chin and looked at him. "It was pretty easy. I never wanted to go all the way with any of my boyfriends. I think it was because my mom had such a great relationship with Frank. I saw that and decided I wanted the same. I wasn't willing to settle on some fumbling in the back of a car with a boy I didn't care about."

If she was trying to make him feel better, she wasn't doing a very good job. "Cynthia, I don't think—"

She reached up and pressed her fingertips to his lips. "Don't worry. I'm not expecting roses and a proposal. What I was trying to say is that I wasn't interested in sex for sex's sake. I wanted my first time to be with the right person. I respect you, Jonathan. I admire you and I think we're good friends. That's why I wanted this."

He stared at her, taking in her wide hazel-green eyes and her pale skin. She was young and beautiful and could he really believe her?

His first thought was no. His second was what on earth was he going to do now?

Then a sharp cry filled the room. They turned toward the sound and he realized it came from the baby monitor.

Cynthia sat up. "Someone is awake and hungry. I'd better go see about that."

She collected her clothes and walked out of the room, leaving Jonathan feeling like he'd both escaped and been dismissed. He wasn't sure which he wanted more.

* * *

Now what? Cynthia wondered as she fed the baby. She'd pulled on a robe and socks, and had taken Colton down to the kitchen. As she held the baby she thought that this wasn't exactly the postromantic moment she'd been thinking about.

"No offense," she told the infant.

Colton didn't bother to respond.

A shadow fell across her. She looked up and saw that Jonathan had entered the kitchen. He'd pulled on jeans and a sweater, but his feet were still bare. The sight of his toes was oddly intimate. She noticed that his hair was mussed and he had a catlike contented quality in his eyes.

Because they'd made love, she thought with some pleasure, and had the sudden desire for them to do it again.

"I don't know what to think," he said, then folded his arms over his chest. "How do you feel about all this?"

I love you.

The words came from nowhere and for a second, Cynthia was afraid that she'd spoken them aloud. But Jonathan's steady gaze didn't alter, so she figured she was safe.

He continued to talk, but she wasn't listening. Instead she thought about those three words and wondered if they were the truth. Did she love him? Is that what this was about? Love? She searched her heart, probing and questioning until the truth appeared with sudden clarity. She *did* love Jonathan. That was the reason she'd wanted to make love with him. She'd wanted to bond with him in the age-old way women had since the beginning of time. She wanted him to be a part of her.

"...and, frankly, I don't know what to do with you," he was saying.

She blinked. "Why do you have to do anything?" She was pleased that her voice sounded so normal. She didn't want him to know what she was thinking. "Can't we continue as we were? Or as we are now?" She felt herself blushing at her forwardness, but didn't look away.

His expression tightened in what she now recognized as desire. "You mean why can't we be lovers?"

"Exactly. I think you liked it and I know I did."

He ran his fingers through his hair and turned away. Bracing his arms against the counter, he dropped his head. "You have no idea what you're saying. This game is beyond you, Cynthia. If you insist on playing, you're going to get hurt."

"I don't think so," she said, struggling to keep her tone light. "I know what I want. And it's you."

He spun to face her. She noticed that he was aroused again. If she wasn't mistaken, there might even be a faint tremor in his hands.

"Don't say that," he growled. "You're out of your league. I'm too old for you."

"Nonsense. If you don't want me, or are afraid, just say so. Don't hide behind excuses."

He surprised her by smiling. "You are always fearless." The smile faded. "This is your last warning. You're not prepared to do this with me."

"I'm a grown woman. I know what I want."

He didn't look convinced. "Let's give it a couple of days. You'll probably find yourself drowning in second thoughts."

"I won't change my mind," she said.

"We'll see."

# *Chapter 11*

Jonathan escaped to the office early Saturday morning, mostly because he couldn't stand being at home with Cynthia. Of course being away from her wasn't that easy, either, so he wasn't able to get a lot of work done. Mostly what he did was pace and think.

Think about what it had been like to make love with her. Think about how soft her skin was and how she tasted and smelled and responded. Of the sweet cries as she climaxed and the way she clung to him. Since they'd made love, he'd spent even more time ready to be with her again. It was as if their single act of love-making had opened a door better left closed. Now he didn't have to imagine what it would be like to be with her. He knew...and it was slowly killing him.

If he was any kind of a decent human being he would find a way to forget what had happened between them and make her forget, too. They were too different to ever have any kind of a relationship and if he didn't figure out how to end it gracefully, Cynthia was going to get hurt.

He might be a real bastard, but he didn't want that. And if there was a way to take back what he'd done— to make her as innocent as she'd been when he'd first met her, he would do it in a heartbeat. No matter the price. He would give up the glory of having been with her to have left her as he'd found her.

He didn't want to be the one she remembered when she thought of the first time because he knew however this ended, it would end badly, and it would be his fault.

He had no experience with a woman like her. Someone who was normal, who had expectations of a forever kind of love and a family. Her world view let her believe that people cared about each other and always did their best, regardless of the personal cost. He believed that everyone was selfish and out for what he could get. There weren't any heroes. Just regular people constantly on the verge of going bad.

And yet he didn't think that about Cynthia. If there was one good person alive, she was the one. He could trust her to lead with her chin and her heart. She wasn't afraid of getting hurt. Hell, she wasn't even afraid of him. She would stand up to him because... He frowned. He didn't know why.

He paced to the window and stared out at the view of Grand Springs. He couldn't change the past, however he might like to, but he could affect the future. He had to promise himself that he would continue to stay away from her. He couldn't touch her again. They could speak about Colton and be pleasant, but no more personal conversations. They would be business associates.

The phone rang. Jonathan turned and stared at the instrument. Tightness gripped his chest. He had a wild and fleeting hope that it was Cynthia calling him. That would be just like her. To demand that he quit hiding and return home to face her like an adult.

He crossed to the desk. A smile tugged at his lips. He could anticipate the frustration in her tone and the way she would be so careful not to call him names, even if she was thinking them. She would rip off his hide...in the politest way possible.

"Steele," he growled into the receiver.

"Don't you sound crabby," a female voice said.

But it wasn't Cynthia and his smile faded. "Hello, Martha Jean."

She sniffed. "Try to sound a little more enthused, darling, or I'll think that you want to get out of our date."

Date? His brain stalled, then retrieved the memory. Of course. They were supposed to go out tonight. "I remember."

"Good. That's the reason I called. I have a silly committee meeting that's going to end with a small cocktail party. So I'll be out and dressed. Instead of you picking me up, why don't I come get you. Then we can return to my place. For dinner."

The last was an afterthought. She wasn't interested in sharing a meal with him and he was supposed to feel exactly the same. He and Martha Jean had always only wanted one thing from each other. Sex.

He tried to picture the raven-haired beauty and could not. He couldn't imagine any other woman except Cynthia. Her hazel eyes and mobile mouth came to him instantly.

"Is seven all right?" she asked.

He wanted to tell her no. He wanted to tell her that he could never be with her again because something had fundamentally changed in his life. He wanted to explain that he'd touched something wonderful and good and because of that he could never touch her again.

Instead he took a deep breath. "Sure. Sounds great."

"See you then, lover."

She hung up. Jonathan stared at the receiver for several seconds, then replaced it. He felt cold and empty, yet he knew he'd done the right thing. Being with Martha Jean would remind him of who he really was. Going out with her after making love with Cynthia made him a real bastard. Cynthia would be hurt, but eventually she would come to see that it was for the best.

He walked back to the window and stared out at the city. He wondered how it was possible to do the right thing and feel that it was incredibly wrong.

Cynthia entered the hall from Colton's room. The baby had just gone down for the night. Now her excuse for being busy was gone and she was left with her thoughts. Unfortunately she was as confused about them as ever.

She didn't know what was happening with Jonathan. He'd been avoiding her ever since they'd made love. He'd buried himself in work and had slipped in and out of the house like a ghost. *She* didn't regret what they'd done, but he was making her feel that he did.

She stood in the center of the hall, not sure what to do next. There was a sound from Jonathan's room, which made the decision for her. She would confront him. If they talked about the problem, surely they could fix it.

She walked to his closed door and knocked firmly. "Jonathan, it's Cynthia. We have to talk."

"Come in."

She drew in a deep breath and turned the handle of the knob. She hadn't been back in this room since they'd made love and she was more than a little concerned about all the memories that awaited her. So instead of looking around the room, she stared at the floor as she entered.

"This is crazy," she said, coming to a stop about five feet from the bed. "We can't keep avoiding each other as if one of us is contagious. I know that you're upset because I was a virgin and you think it's a big deal. I guess I should have told you, but I was afraid of your reaction. Besides, the fact that I picked you to be my first time should be a little flattering, if nothing else. But I meant what I said before. I don't have a lot of expectations." She raised her gaze to look at him. "No, I take that back. I do have one expectation."

Words fled her. She opened her mouth, but nothing came out. Jonathan stood in the doorway to his private bath. He'd obviously showered and shaved. He wore an elegant dark suit. Not the casual clothes he usually wore when he was home.

He stared at her, his face unreadable. "What is your expectation?"

"That, ah, that we maintain our friendship. I hate that you're avoiding me." Her chest felt funny. Tight, but it was more than that. She couldn't seem to breathe. "Are you going out?" she asked, her voice barely audible.

"Yes."

His curt response cut through her. She had to bite on her lower lip to keep from crying out. She took a step back. "I—I don't understand. It's a business dinner, right? You can't mean on a *date*."

"That's exactly what I mean." He walked to his dresser where he slipped on his watch, then tucked his wallet into his jacket pocket. "I made these arrangements some time ago and I can't cancel them now."

"But, I don't understand."

He turned to face her. His gaze hardened. "No, you don't. That was my point. You say that you're willing to play my kind of game, but you're not."

Pain blossomed inside of her. It grew and flowered until there wasn't room for anything else. He was going out with another woman. They were going to be together. At dinner, possibly dancing…making love.

The vision of him with someone else filled her brain. The need to cry out was almost primal. She wanted to run and hide, but where was there to go? She wanted to attack him, to pummel him, to scream that he didn't have the right to treat her this way.

But she didn't do any of those things. Not with him watching her, waiting for her to act like the innocent young woman she was. He expected her to fall apart and that expectation gave her the courage to be strong.

"Stop looking at me like that," he growled. "I told you I wasn't a saint."

"I certainly believe you now," she managed to say. The doorbell rang.

"That would be my family," she said. "Tonight is Jenny's dance. My mom said they'd all come by so I could see her. If you'll excuse me."

She forced herself to turn and walk away even though it felt as if a thousand shards of glass were cutting through her body. She didn't know what to say or how to act, so in the end, she simply put one foot in front of the other and made her way down the stairs.

Another woman. There was another woman. All this

time she'd thought that Jonathan was closed off from the world. That he didn't believe in anyone or anything. That he needed her to emotionally take care of him the way that Colton needed her to physically take care of him. When all the time he'd been seeing someone else. She'd assumed he was broken and that she in her wisdom could heal him.

She'd been a fool. Worse, she'd made a fool of herself. He wasn't worried about not being worthy of being her first time. He was terrified that she wouldn't recognize a one-night stand when it happened. He thought that she expected more of him than he wanted to give. It wasn't that he wasn't capable, it was that he wasn't interested.

Humiliation added to her pain. As she reached the front door, she tried to compose herself so that her family wouldn't know that something was wrong. She wasn't sure she was successful.

"Hi," she said with a false brightness as she pulled open the door. Jenny, her mother and the twins stood on the wide front porch. But none of them were smiling.

At first Cynthia couldn't figure out the problem, then someone moved in front of her family—a tall, dark-haired woman with incredible green eyes and a form-fitting black dress that left little to the imagination.

Cynthia stared at her. It was her worst nightmare. It was worse than just about anything in her life, except Frank's death.

The woman didn't just have an amazing body. She was also beautiful enough to inspire a revolution. Her haughty gaze settled on Cynthia. "I didn't realize Jonathan had a new housekeeper. Shouldn't you be in uniform?"

With that, the woman pushed past Cynthia and entered the house. "Tell Jonathan I'm here. I'm Martha Jean Porter."

She spoke the name as if it meant something. Cynthia blinked at her.

"She's not the housekeeper, Martha Jean."

Jonathan had come down the stairs and joined them. He nodded at Cynthia. "Please invite your family inside."

Cynthia realized she was still standing in front of the door. She stepped back. Her mother and the children took hesitant steps into the impressive foyer.

"Cynthia Morgan is my nephew's nanny," Jonathan said by way of introduction. "This is her mother, Betsy Morgan, her sister Jenny, and those two rug rats are Brett and Brad."

He smiled at the boys, but the twins only moved closer to Betsy. "Why does she smell funny?" Brett asked in a too-loud whisper.

Martha Jean stiffened. Then she slid next to Jonathan and tucked her arm through the crook of his elbow. "You let your hired help entertain? Jonathan, I would have expected better of you."

Cynthia didn't know what to say. Jonathan rescued her by stepping in.

"Jenny has her first school dance tonight. They just stopped by to show her off." He turned his attention to the teenager. "Remember what I said about the boys? It's doubly true tonight."

Jenny blushed. For the first time Cynthia was able to notice what her sister looked like. Betsy had piled her long blond hair on top of her head in a cascade of curls. A cream-colored dress fell in layers to midcalf. Cynthia looked closer then laughed and hugged her sister.

"I recognize my old prom dress," she murmured in

her ear. "I hate that it looks better on you than it did on me."

Jenny hugged her back. "That's not true but thank you for pretending it is."

"I'm sure she looks as lovely as possible," Martha Jean said in an obviously bored voice. "Can we leave now?"

Jonathan didn't protest as the beauty led him from his house. Cynthia could only watch helplessly as they disappeared into the night. The pain inside of her was as strong as ever and she had a fleeting thought that while it might not kill her, it could certainly destroy her.

She turned and caught her mother's knowing gaze. She flushed. How much had Betsy guessed?

"I had a plan," her mother said. "I thought I'd leave the boys with you while I take Jenny to the middle school. You three can argue about which pizza to order. After dinner, I thought we'd watch a movie. The twins picked out a couple at the video store."

Cynthia nodded. "Sounds great," she said, wondering if she would be able to eat or if the food would choke her. She wasn't hungry. She didn't think she would ever be hungry again.


Dinner consisted of a small salad followed by crab in a pastry shell and a few vegetables. Martha Jean kept the conversation moving along topics of mutual interest such as business and people in town.

Jonathan listened with half an ear and picked at his food. Not that it wasn't tasty, but he wasn't in the mood for a meal designed to give him energy without making him feel too full to perform. Martha Jean was many things, but subtle wasn't one of them. Even now, as they talked about investment opportunities brought on by a building boom, she reached across the small table to rest her fingertips on the back of his hand. Her nails scraped across his skin in a way designed to arouse and intrigue.

He wondered if he should tell her that it wasn't working. Was it her or was it him? He and Martha Jean had been lovers on and off for years. When she was between men, she liked to come calling and so far he'd never told her no. She was good in bed and uncomplicated. What was there not to like?

But tonight something was different. He remembered Brett's comment about her perfume and couldn't help agreeing with the boy. Her scent was cloying, seeming to fill the room and almost attack him. And could her dress be more obvious? The black fabric was so tight, he was surprised that she could eat anything without popping out of it. He compared her complicated and sophisticated hairstyle with a ponytail and found the former lacking.

She'd always made it easy because she didn't want to get involved any more than he did. But now he couldn't see what was so special about that.

"Your little nanny was interesting," Martha Jean said as she picked up her glass of wine. "Very homespun. Does her family intrude often?"

"No, but I enjoy their company."

"Really?" Dark eyebrows rose in an expression of surprise. "Well, at least you have the problem of your nephew solved with minimal inconvenience."

Her attitude couldn't have been more different from Cynthia's. "How is it you've never had children?" he asked. "All those husbands and none of them wanted an heir?"

She leaned back in her chair and laughed. "Of course they *wanted* children. So many men are funny that way. But I have no intention of getting pregnant. Do you know what that sort of thing does to a woman's body? It's disgusting."

She rose to her feet and came around to stand behind his chair. She pressed herself to him, then kissed his neck. "Unless we're talking about your child, my love. I would be willing to do many things to have *your* baby."

He wasn't fooled for a second. "You think I'm that rich?"

She chuckled warmly and licked his ear. "I know you are. Any woman would do just about anything for you, darling. Why should I be an exception? After all, I have the advantage of knowing that money isn't even your best asset." She slipped one hand down to his crotch. "I've been with more than my share of men and I have to admit, you're in the top ten percent."

He tossed his napkin on the table and rose to his feet. "How flattering."

Martha Jean moved close, a smile tugging on her lips. She stopped a foot in front of him and unzipped her dress. The slinky garment fell to the floor.

Jonathan watched it go, then stared at her perfect body clad only in a strapless bra, panties, garter belt and stockings. Nothing about her moved him. He found himself remembering someone very different. Someone charming and sincere, and completely uninterested in his money or doing what he wanted. Someone who did what was right. Suddenly he didn't know what the hell he was doing here.

"I have to go," he said, and walked to the phone.

He dialed information and asked for a cab company, then had them connect him with the number.

"What are you doing?" Martha Jean demanded when he hung up. "You're leaving? But we haven't done it yet."

"I know." He stared at her. "I'm sorry, but this relationship isn't going to work anymore."

She glared at him. "How dare you leave me? You're here to take care of my needs. Damn you, Jonathan, I waited two weeks for this night and you're not going until you've done what we both want. What on earth is wrong with you?"

He walked to the door. "It's rather strange," he told her. "I've realized that I'm developing standards and you're not up to mine."

Cynthia and her mother sat on the living-room sofa while the twins watched a movie in the den. The pizza was history, although Cynthia hadn't been able to do more than nibble on half a piece.

"Want to talk about it?" Betsy asked. "And don't say you don't know what I mean. You've barely spoken, you didn't eat your dinner and you look as if you've been shot."

Cynthia shook her head. What was she supposed to say? That she was a fool? That she'd believed in something that didn't exist? That she'd given her heart to a man who didn't care about her at all?

"I know it's Jonathan," Betsy said quietly. She placed her hand on her daughter's forearm. "I tried to warn you before, honey. He's not your type. He's too old and too experienced in the ways of the world. If you insist on falling for him, you're going to get hurt."

"Too late for both," she whispered and tried to fake a smile. "Oh, well."

Betsy looked stricken, then leaned toward her and pulled her close. "I'm so sorry." She hugged Cynthia and rocked slightly, as she had when her daughter had been a young girl. "Is there anything I can do?"

Cynthia tightly closed her eyes and tried not to cry. Crying would only make it worse. Right now the pain made it nearly impossible to breathe, but if she gave in to tears, it would grow and consume her. She had to maintain control at any cost.

"This is all my fault," Betsy said. "It's Frank. You saw how we loved each other and wanted that same thing for yourself. You never dated much. I didn't worry about it but I see now that I should have."

Cynthia raised her head and stared at her mother. "Because I wanted what you had? Is that so bad?"

"Because you weren't willing to settle for anything else. You needed to be meeting all kinds of boys and trying to figure out which ones were for you. Instead you set your sights on an impossible dream. You've fallen in love with him, haven't you?"

Cynthia nodded. "It doesn't matter. He doesn't love me back."

"Oh, honey. I'm so sorry." Her mother stroked her back. "I know you don't want to hear this now, but it will get better with time. The wounds will heal and you'll be able to start over. Just promise me that next time you'll stick with someone your own age. Someone with your own level of experience."

She couldn't imagine a next time. She'd barely given her heart away, only to have it returned all smashed and burned. Why on earth would she want to do that again?

Jonathan walked into the quiet house close to midnight. He'd had the first cab drop him off at the office so that he could think, then he'd called for a second one to take him home. He supposed that he was a coward along with a jerk, because in the back of his mind he knew that he'd been avoiding an encounter with Cynthia's family. He didn't want them knowing how he'd hurt her.

Not that he could expect them to stay in ignorance for very long. Betsy probably already knew what he'd done to her daughter. He stood in the darkened foyer and wondered how he could justify his actions. Then he knew he couldn't. What he'd done was wrong. All of it.

He shouldn't have made love with her, he should have stopped when he realized she was a virgin. Once that was done, he should have handled the situation differently afterward. He should have held her close and made her feel good about what they'd done. He should have sat down with her and talked until she understood the ramifications of what had happened. Together they should have redefined their relationship.

Instead he'd turned his back on her and ignored her. He'd hurt her desperately by going out with Martha Jean. Was there even one thing he hadn't screwed up?

Jonathan couldn't think of it, so he made his way to the stairs. He might not be able to change the past, but he could improve the future. The first thing he had to do was apologize. The second was to find out what she needed from him and do his best to provide it. Unfortunately, while Martha Jean wasn't up to his standards, he wasn't even close to Cynthia's. Still, he was all she had right now.

He was going to have to make her see that she would be better off without him. That in time she would find a nice young man who still believed in all the things she did. Someone with whom she could have a future.

At the top of the stairs, he walked toward her room. As he got closer, he heard the sharp sound of a sob. It ripped through him, making him clench his hands into fists. He'd done that to her. He was to blame.

He'd been wrong to go out with Martha Jean. That had been the coward's way out. Cynthia wouldn't have done it. She was brave enough to face the consequences of her actions, regardless of what they might be. She was stronger than anyone he'd ever known. He admired her and wanted her. And he would prove his respect and admiration by never touching her again.

But first, he had to fix what he'd done wrong.

# Chapter 12

Cynthia closed her eyes against the pain that filled her. Tears continued to spill down her face and she didn't know how to make them stop. She'd told herself earlier that if she gave in and started crying, she would never be able to stop. Unfortunately she'd been right.

She loved him and he'd left her. She loved him and he'd gone to be with another woman. Right now he could be in her bed doing all those things with her that he'd done with Cynthia. That's what hurt the most. Not his potential infidelity, but that when he'd been making love with her it hadn't meant anything. If it had, he wouldn't have been able to go to another woman's bed so quickly and easily. She hadn't been a person to Jonathan, she'd been a body.

She drew her knees to her chest and held her pillow tighter. Her mother had tried to warn her that he wasn't for her. She tried to tell herself. But then she'd blindly fallen in love with him. As if she had a chance to make it work with a man like him. As if this really was a fairy tale and she was Cinderella and the handsome prince was going to make everything work out all right.

The pain inside of her grew until it threatened to consume her. She couldn't breathe anymore. In an effort to gain control she told herself that the hurt didn't matter, but she knew it did. She had responsibilities. However much she might be hurt now, she had a life she had to live. Somehow she needed to find the strength to see Jonathan again and do it in such a way that he wouldn't know she'd been the least bit upset by what had happened tonight. She needed to face him with cool confidence, the veneer of sophistication firmly in place. He probably expected her to act like a child, but she would be the adult in the relationship. With her head held high.

In the morning she would get up and look him and the world in the eye. She would be strong. But for tonight, while she was all alone, she needed to lie here and ache.

A splash of light cut across her tightly closed eyes. She sensed and shifted, then looked up. Much to her horror, Jonathan stood standing in the doorway of her bedroom. She gulped back a sob and wondered what she was supposed to say or do. It was one thing to plan on a coolly, confident entrance to fool him, it was another to be caught in the middle of a heart-wrenching tearfest.

"I'm sorry," he said quietly. "About a lot of things. I'm sorry I didn't know you were a virgin. I would have done things differently."

"No," she said, her voice thick with tears. "You wouldn't have done anything at all. You would have run far and fast in the opposite direction."

"Maybe. Or I might have taken things more slowly, making your first time better for you."

She blinked. Tears cleared from her eyes and he swam back in focus. Better? Was that possible? "I don't want to talk about that."

"What about my apology for not holding you?" he asked. "I should have done that after we made love. My only excuse is that I was so surprised to find out the truth that I panicked. Twenty-six-year-old virgins aren't something a man runs into every day."

She sniffed. "I guess not."

He took a step toward her. Light from the hallway spilled into the room, illuminating him in silhouette. She could see the shape of his body, but not his face or his expression. Unfortunately he could see her clearly, in all her puffy, blotchy glory. She flopped onto her back and stared at the ceiling. Life was not fair.

"I also want to apologize for tonight," he said, moving farther into the room. "I'd made plans with Martha Jean a couple of weeks ago. To be honest, I'd forgotten about them. After you and I made love, I was concerned about..." His voice trailed off. He sat on the edge of the bed and looked at her. "I had several concerns," he amended. "Going out with her seemed to address a lot of them. However, it was wrong and the coward's way out."

She brushed the tears from her cheeks. "Is she..." Cynthia wasn't sure what she wanted to ask, let alone how to phrase the question. "Is she important to you?"

He paused before speaking. He was close enough that she could see his determined expression. It was as if he had an agenda for their conversation and had every intention to get through it.

"Not in the way you mean. I've known Martha Jean

for years. Her hobby is marrying wealthy men and then divorcing them. We get involved when she's between husbands or fiancés. I find her uncomplicated. But tonight, it got complicated with her. Mostly because of you."

"You don't like a lot of complication in your life, do you?"

"It's something I avoid at all costs," he admitted, then traced the curve of her cheek with one finger. "You are a complication I didn't expect and therefore forgot to avoid." He hesitated. "Cynthia, you're a bright, beautiful young woman. You have definite world views which I do not share. You see the best in people. I would imagine that one of your greatest goals is to marry and have a family."

Her mind lingered on the word "beautiful" and she wanted to know if that was really how he saw her. Of course she couldn't ask. "Don't most people want to get married and have a family?"

"I suppose they do. But I've managed to avoid both for many years and I'm not likely to change that now."

"But you already have. What about Colton?"

He stared at her as if her question had stumped him. "That's different."

"Like it or not, you have a family, Jonathan. You're a father."

He stiffened slightly and withdrew his hand. "That's not the point. What I'm trying to say is that you need to find a man who is more like you. Someone who shares your world views. Someone optimistic and young."

"What does age have to do with anything?"

"More than you realize. I can't be what you need me to be."

''That's interesting because I don't even know what I need right now,'' she admitted. Some of the pain in her chest had eased. Obviously Jonathan hadn't intended to hurt her. He'd been trying to escape. But from what?

''Did you and Martha Jean, um, well... Were you two, ah, intimate tonight?'' she asked.

He held her gaze. ''No.''

Relief filled her, chasing away the last of the pain. ''Good,'' she whispered.

''No,'' he said sharply. ''Not good. Not good at all. I should have had sex with Martha Jean because we both need to know that there is no connection between you and me.''

''A connection?'' A faint tickling began on the inside of her chest. Hope, she thought. Or at least a lessening of despair. ''You felt we connected when we made love?''

''Not exactly,'' he hedged. ''It was different from that. But it wasn't just sex, either. Which is what it needs to be.''

Definitely hope, she thought dreamily as she pushed herself into a sitting position. ''Why? Why can't we have made love and connected?''

He glared at her. ''Have you been listening? I'm absolutely the wrong man for you. Nothing about this is going to work. I'll only end up hurting you more.'' He grabbed her upper arms and pushed her away. ''Quit looking at me like that. I'm not anyone you should care about or trust. You work for me. I will not take advantage of that.''

He said all the right things, but she could see the fire in his eyes and feel the heat radiating from him. His lips told her no, but his body screamed that he wanted her as much as she wanted him.

"I don't think you'd be taking advantage of me," she said. "Not if I was a willing participant. You keep thinking of me as a young, inexperienced girl. While I'll admit that I haven't been with a lot of different men, I'm not that young. I've been a legal adult for years."

He stood up. "This is crazy."

"I know, but that doesn't change how I feel." She slid to the edge of the bed and rose to her feet.

He took a step back. "I've warned you, Cynthia. I'm not the right man for you. If you think I hurt you tonight, you're not even close to imagining the pain I could bring you. You want me to be a saint, but if I have any likeness to a supernatural being, put me on the side of the devil."

"I don't think the devil would work so hard to save an innocent. And that's what you're doing...trying to save me from yourself. But it's not necessary. I'm stronger than you think. I can take care of myself and protect myself."

Cheap talk coming from someone who had spent the last hour and a half in tears, she thought briefly, then dismissed the warning. Her mind, her body, even her soul was not her own anymore. She'd lost the power to walk away from this man, if she'd ever had it at all. What she knew was that he wanted her and that he would fight that wanting because he thought it was the right thing to do.

Didn't he know that his nobility only made her love him more?

"You want me," she breathed.

He swore. The harsh, guttural words should have

frightened or offended her, but they did neither. She smiled.

"I would have expected something more original," she teased. "Or at least something more eloquent."

"How's this?" he asked as he moved toward her.

His arms came around her and his mouth claimed hers. She went willingly, losing herself in his kiss and his embrace.

His body was warm and solid against her own. His familiar scent surrounded her, making her feel safe and arousing her. She thought about all they'd done together last time and desperately wanted to do it all again.

His tongue swept across her bottom lip. She opened for him, but he didn't enter. Instead he straightened and looked at her. "I can taste your tears," he said hoarsely. "I'm so sorry. The hell of it is I can't promise not to make you cry again."

"I'll take my chances," she said lightly.

"You shouldn't. You should run." He dropped his hands to his sides. "I'm not going to do anything to convince you to stay."

"You don't have to," she told him, then wrapped her arms around his neck and pressed her mouth to his. "I want you," she whispered.

He shuddered, then hauled her hard against him. This time his tongue plunged into her mouth, touching and tasting and taking. It was a demanding kiss, a *man's* kiss. She reveled in his passion, his need, pleased that she was able to bring him to such a frenzied state.

His hands were everywhere. On her back, her arms, then reaching around and cupping her breasts. Now it was her turn to shudder and shiver as he teased her nipples into tight peaks.

Desire filled her, making her ache all over. Every

millimeter of her skin grew tight and sensitized. When he backed her toward the bed, she went willingly, still kissing him deeply.

He murmured something against her mouth. She didn't catch the words, but she knew what he was saying. That he wanted this, wanted *her*. She would have returned the compliment if she'd been able to, but she couldn't stop what she was doing long enough to speak.

She clung to his shoulders then moved her hands down his back. His muscles jumped in response. She cupped his rear and felt him flex against her. The hardness of his arousal brushed against her belly. Her body leaped in response. She needed him as much as she needed to breathe. Nothing else mattered.

Still kissing her, he tugged at the hem of her sweatshirt. They were forced to part so that he could pull off the garment. Then he laughed and swore. "We might as well get naked now," he said, reaching for her jeans.

While he expertly unfastened the zipper, then removed her bra, she found herself barely able to undo a single button on his shirt. It wasn't just that his hands and arms were in the way as he removed her clothing. It was that she trembled so much she couldn't force the small white buttons through the openings. Finally he pushed her hands away and quickly began removing his own clothing.

Cynthia, already topless, with her jeans barely clinging to her hips, decided to pretend to be brave. She shoved down her pants and panties, then stepped out of them. When she was naked, she stood and waited for Jonathan to notice. By then he'd taken off his shirt, socks and shoes and was just stepping out of his trousers. Her gaze settled on the hardness trapped by his briefs and she found herself unable to move.

Unaware of her interest, he hooked his thumbs inside the wide band of elastic and pulled off his underwear. When he straightened, she stared at that most male part of him. The part she'd only caught a glimpse of the last time they'd made love.

"You've never seen a man before, have you?" he asked gruffly.

She looked up and blushed, then shook her head. "Sorry."

"Don't apologize." He stood in front of her but didn't move. "Go ahead. Get used to it. You can even touch me if you'd like."

A hint of laughter laced his words. She bit her lower lip, then slowly reached out to touch him.

He was big, she thought, wondering how he'd been able to fit himself inside of her. She remembered a stretching sensation but it hadn't been unpleasant. Perhaps with time she would grow more comfortable and he would fill her easily.

Gently she brushed the top of him with her fingertips. She hadn't been sure what to expect, but was pleased to find him both warm and dry to the touch. The skin was surprisingly soft, although the organ itself was tight and hard. Tentatively she closed her hand around him and rubbed. He groaned.

Her gaze flew to his face. "Did I hurt you?" she asked, releasing him instantly.

"You're killing me, but that isn't what you were asking," he said and kissed her. "Hold that thought."

Before she knew what was happening, he'd left. She stood alone in the semidarkness. Had she really hurt him? Had she said the wrong thing or broken the mood or had he changed his mind or...

Jonathan returned with a condom in his hand. "Protection,'' he said and set it on the nightstand. Then he moved next to her and took her in his arms.

While they kissed, he urged her back on the bed. Soon she was stretched out on the mattress with his body pressing against hers. He kissed her mouth, then moved lower, trailing down her chin to her throat. Her skin felt both hot and cold. Shivers rippled through her. As he approached her breasts, she found herself arching in anticipation. She clutched the bedspread, desperate to have him touch her chest—the way he had before. She wanted his mouth, his lips, on her nipples. She wanted to feel that exquisite tugging as he drew the tight peaks into his mouth and nibbled so lightly.

Just thinking about it was enough to make her legs fall open. Heat and dampness swelled inside of her. Soon he would be thrusting himself there and she found she couldn't wait.

But then he reached her breasts. He touched and teased. With lips, tongue and fingers, he made her toss her head from side to side and call out his name. He drove her to the edge of paradise. Between her thighs, pressure built until she knew it wouldn't take but a moment of touching to allow her to climax.

Still kissing her breasts, he shifted until he was between her legs. His mouth moved lower, down her belly. He lingered at her belly button, teasing her with quick licks that made her giggle. The giggle became a gasp as he settled his hands on her thighs and began to rub the sensitized flesh there.

He moved up in sweeping movements that brought him perilously close to her feminine place, but he didn't touch it. Closer and closer, until she thought the heat might consume her. At last he slipped between the protective folds and drew them apart. Then he dipped his head and kissed her there.

Cynthia's eyes shot open, but she couldn't see very much in the darkened room. She wasn't sure what to think about what he was doing. It felt so...so... Incredible.

His tongue stroked that tiny point of pleasure and she thought she might die. Instinctively she drew her knees up and out, opening herself to him. As he kissed and licked and explored, her body began to melt from the inside. She dug her heels into the mattress; her hips arched toward him.

"Don't stop," she gasped, knowing that if he did, she would die. It was too intense, too wonderful. She couldn't possibly climax this way—not if she meant to survive.

But she couldn't stand for him to stop, either. And when he slipped a single finger inside of her and began to caress that sacred place from underneath, she completely lost control. Passion rushed through her, over her, taking her apart in the most perfect way possible.

When the last of the ripples had faded and she could only tremble, he gathered her in his arms and held her close.

"How is that possible?" she asked.

He didn't answer. Instead he stroked her hair and rocked her until she quieted.

Eventually she noticed the rather large male object butting into her thigh. She reached down and touched him.

"About your friend here," she teased.

Jonathan smiled. "He's being rather insistent."

"I don't mind that. Why don't we see if we can find a way to make him happy."

He reached for the protection and drew it on. "I have a couple of suggestions," he said, moving between her knees and pressing into her.

"I'll just bet you do," she gasped as her body stretched to welcome him.

This felt so right, she thought as the passion began to grow again. She wanted this man inside of her, claiming her in the ancient way that men had always claimed women. As he moved, she felt herself tensing. Passion built. Faster and faster. She concentrated on his strength, the weight of him, the way his dark gaze locked with hers.

It began again, she thought, stunned as need filled her and ripped through her.

"Yes," he growled triumphantly as she clung to him.

She grabbed his hips, urging him deeper. Her body tensed, then released as pleasure washed over her. He thrust harder and faster, each moment of penetration even more satisfying than the one before. Only after she'd climaxed three more times did he give into his own pleasure and grow still within her. Their gasping breaths mingled as they kissed in a moment of exquisite union.

That night, as Jonathan had told himself he should have done the first time, he held her. They lay in a tangle of arms and legs that spoke of their lovers' celebration. He'd tried to tell her that he wasn't right for her, but she hadn't listened. He'd tried to walk away from her, but he hadn't been able to do that, either. So now while she slept, he stared into the darkness and wondered what he was supposed to do next. How could he get away from a woman when he didn't want her out of his life? And if he asked her to stay, what on earth was he going to do with her?

Jack Stryker and Max Shelton, David and Lisa's lawyer, sat across from Jonathan. It was midafternoon on Monday and the two men were there to discuss important business. Unfortunately Jonathan found himself unable to focus on what they were talking about.

For the first time in his life, his personal relationships were interfering with work. He'd come into the office prepared to work and all morning he'd accomplished less than nothing. What was wrong with him?

But even as he asked the question, he knew the answer. It had something to do with a pair of hazel-green eyes and a smile sweet enough to reform the devil...or maybe even a man like himself. Instead of getting up Sunday morning and establishing a little distance between himself and Cynthia, he'd lingered in her bed. They'd spent the day together. He'd even helped her with Colton, something he still couldn't believe that had happened. And last night they'd made love over and over until he hadn't wanted to leave her side this morning.

He was in deep and he didn't know what to do about it.

"So we have a missing killer," Stryker was saying, "and a guy who doesn't remember anything. Or so he claims."

Jonathan forced himself to pay attention to the conversation. "You don't believe him?"

"I don't know. It's damn convenient. He's involved *somehow*. But on which side? We know David and Lisa had a contact who is probably the killer. Tom Flynt—

the guy who lost his memory—may be an accomplice, a concerned citizen, or who knows what."

Stryker shifted in his seat. "We want to go through David and Lisa's papers. There's the issue of client-lawyer privilege and we were hoping you would smooth things over with Mr. Shelton."

"You think you'll find some answers about Tom Flynt?"

"We hope."

Jonathan glanced at the slick lawyer in his three-thousand-dollar suit. He'd never been a fan of Shelton's but the man was efficient. Jonathan was Colton's legal guardian and Colton was the sole heir of the estate. Therefore some attorney-client privilege extended to Colton, through Jonathan.

Jonathan thought about all his brother had done. He suspected there were more crimes he couldn't even begin to imagine. What did it matter if they all came to light now?

"Give them whatever they want," he told Shelton. "Papers, contracts, anything there is. I don't want any secrets."

Shelton raised his eyebrows. "You could be jeopardizing part of your nephew's estate."

"He's not going to need the money. I have more than enough."

Stryker looked pleased. "I'll let the FBI know." He rose. "Let me go make the call right now."

After he left, Shelton stared at Jonathan. "As you requested, I've made arrangements to have your brother's property liquidated. The house and its contents will be inventoried at the end of the week. I suggest you go through it one more time to see if there's anything you want to keep either for yourself or the child."

Jonathan started to tell him that he wasn't interested in anything of David's but then he thought about Colton. While he might not know what would be of future interest to David's son, Cynthia would. She could help him make the right choices for the boy so that he could have a connection to his past…however tenuous.

"I'll get over there before Friday," he promised.

He and Shelton talked over a few more items of business, then the man left. When Jonathan was alone, he tried to return his attention to his work, but all he could think about was Cynthia. Even though they'd made love the previous night, he found himself wanting her again. Somehow in the middle of all this, he'd lost control. He'd better find it and quick, before he did something stupid—like starting to imagine they could ever make this work.

# Chapter 13

Jonathan let himself in the front door of the house. Light spilled into the darkened foyer from the living room. The double doors stood open and the sound of music drifted toward him.

He set down his briefcase and shrugged out of his coat. On an impulse, he'd called Cynthia late that afternoon and told her what time he would be home. *She'd* told *him* to expect a surprise. Now as he stared at the light reflecting on the black-and-white marble floor, he wondered what she had in store for him. He also wondered when he'd gotten soft.

While he would rather eat glass than admit it, a part of him enjoyed knowing that she and Colton were at home waiting for him. All his life he'd come home to an empty house. He usually got home so late that even Lucinda was gone. She left him a plate of food and instructions for warming, but that was his sole contact with humanity outside of the office. When he was involved with a woman, he made it a point to see her at her place, rather than his. In the past he'd always told himself that he liked the solitude. Now he wasn't so sure.

Jonathan crossed the floor, moving quietly so he could catch them unaware. He wanted a moment to observe Cynthia and the baby, although he couldn't say why. The situation should make him uncomfortable, and in a way it did. Yet it also felt right, despite the fact that he hadn't been able to work all day for thinking about her and how they'd spent the weekend together.

He reached the doorway of the living room. Cynthia and Colton were on a blanket in the middle of the floor. A fire burned cheerfully in the oversize fireplace on the opposite wall. As she'd done when she'd taught her sister to dance, Cynthia had pushed most of the furniture out of the way. Next to her was a low table with several covered dishes and an ice bucket filled with a bottle of wine.

Colton lay on his stomach. His stocking-clad feet kicked in delight as he giggled at Cynthia. Jonathan didn't think the baby knew him from a rock, but Colton raised his head and saw him, smiled, then waved a pudgy, baby arm in his direction. Cynthia turned and saw him. She smiled as well, then rose and walked over to him.

"You're home," she said with obvious delight. "We were just talking about how hungry we are and how exciting the picnic is going to be."

She stepped into an embrace he hadn't meant to offer. But as he hugged her close, then kissed her, the moment felt right. Her familiar body pressed against his in a way that had him counting the hours until Colton went to bed. She tilted her head back to study him.

"How was your day?" she asked as she took his hand and led him over to the blanket.

"Good."

"That's what I like to hear."

She urged him to sit on the blanket. It was surprisingly soft and he noticed that she'd put a couple of down comforters underneath for cushioning.

He spent his day surrounded by professionals, many of them women. He was used to seeing the females in his life dressed in suits or career dresses. As usual, Cynthia wore jeans and a sweater. Light makeup accentuated her hazel-green eyes, but any lipstick was long gone. She looked fresh and lovely and impossibly young. He knew he had no business messing with her or her life. If he was any kind of a decent human being, he would end this. But he couldn't. Not yet.

"I thought we'd dine alfresco," she said, motioning to the plates of food on the table. "Sort of a celebration."

He took in the bright flowers in vases set strategically beside the table and the red-and-white checkered napkins by the plates. "A picnic?" he asked. "It's November and it's raining."

"Not in here," she said with a smile.

"But alfresco means 'outside.'"

"If you're going to get wildly technical, you'll have to eat alone."

The laughter in her eyes belied her stern tone. He found himself relaxing and enjoying her company. "Yes, ma'am."

"That's more like it." She pointed to the wine. "Why don't you go ahead and open that. I'll start serving the food. Colton's eaten already so he'll just be watching."

By the time he'd poured them each a glass of the smooth Chardonnay, she'd filled a plate for both of them. Jonathan couldn't remember the last time he'd had dinner on the floor, but he was surprisingly comfortable with the arrangement. Colton found the simplest objects endlessly fascinating. He cooed over a set of keys, then went into baby rapture at the sight of an empty plate that doubled as a mirror.

Cynthia kept one eye on the infant as she ate her dinner. "You said your day was fine," she said. "Do you want to go into detail on that?"

Jonathan hesitated. "Detective Stryker was by updating me on the case. The police want to go through all of David's papers. Max Shelton, David's lawyer was at the meeting as well. I told him to give the police anything they wanted. Even the things that are still covered by attorney-client privilege." He took a bite of cold chicken and chewed. "David's house is being inventoried at the end of the week. I want everything sold. The money will go in a trust for Colton."

She looked at him, her expression sad. "I know that he's not going to need the money. You'll more than take care of him." She paused. "You're sure about selling the house?"

"You've seen it. Do you think it's the right place to raise a small child?"

Cynthia shook her head. "No. It was cold and made me uncomfortable. Even Colton's room wasn't all that welcoming."

"I'm going to make a trip over there tomorrow afternoon," he said. "I've thought about what you said before—about saving some things for Colton." He shrugged. "As much as I didn't get along with my brother, I realize it's important for Colton to have some link with his past.''

"I'll go with you," she told him. "That is if you want me along." She held up a hand. "Before you automatically say no, consider the fact that even though you and David had some issues, he was still your brother and the house will remind you of him. It might be easier to have company."

Cynthia spoke sincerely and he believed her. She led with her heart. He couldn't remember the last time someone had offered to help, just to make a situation easier for him. Of course he had a staff at work and their jobs were to offer different kinds of support, but nothing like this.

"I'd like the company," he said.

"Good." She dazzled him with a smile. "I'll leave Colton with Lucinda. That will make it easier for us to get things done and will make her afternoon." She took a sip of wine. "Jonathan, you don't have to answer this if you don't want to, but why didn't you get along with your father?"

He put down his plate. The smell of wood smoke drifted into the room. The sound of rain tapped against the windows. The night might be wet and cold, but here in the house, they were snug and warm. He thought about her question. If anyone else had asked, he wouldn't have bothered answering. But this was Cynthia and she wasn't curious, she was concerned. Odd how lately he'd learned the difference.

"My mother ran off when I was five," he said at last. "She abandoned both me and my father. For some reason, he thought it was my fault. I never knew why. But from then on, he wouldn't forgive me for being her son. I still lived in this house, but I could have been a ghost for all the notice he took of me.''

Cynthia stared at him. "I don't understand."

"You and me both." He took a sip of wine, then focused his attention on Colton. It was easier to look at the baby than see the pity in Cynthia's eyes. "My father remarried fairly quickly. Within a year, he had a new son. David was the golden boy. From then on, I couldn't do anything right and David couldn't do anything wrong."

"But I've read your bio. You got terrific grades in school and were a star athlete. You turned down full scholarships to several universities because you could afford to pay your own way. You took your father's company forward, changing it from a medium size, nearly failing firm into a multinational, I-don't-know-how-many billion dollar success."

He returned his attention to her and smiled. "Let me know if you want a job in my PR department."

She shook her head. "I'm being serious. Are you saying that he never once acknowledged any of your accomplishments simply because he couldn't forgive your mother?"

"Yes."

The single word hung between them.

"It doesn't matter," he finally said. "I let it go a long time ago."

"I don't believe you." She frowned. "Parents' opinions matter, even when we don't want them to. I think we're hard-wired to need their approval and love."

"It's a nonissue for me," he insisted. "As for the love part, that goes along with your Pollyanna attitude about families. Nice, but not necessary."

"You can pretend all you want," she said, "but I'm

not buying it. However much you want to claim you
don't care or need love, it's not true. Everyone needs a
connection."

"I've survived very nicely for thirty-seven years."

She glanced at the baby. "What about Colton? Don't
you care about him?"

He hesitated. They were getting into dangerous ter-
ritory. He knew what she wanted him to say, but he
wasn't going to lie to please her.

"Jonathan?" Her voice was low and pleading. "You
have to believe you'll come to love him."

"Why?" He set down his wine and leaned toward
her. "I've told you not to try to make me more than I
am, Cynthia. Just a man. Not a saint or the devil. I have
some flaws. I'll admit mine are probably bigger than
most, but I've learned to live with that."

"No, you're more than that."

Her belief in him was painful. He found himself
wanting to believe in himself the way she believed in
him, but he knew it was all just illusion. Just like love
itself.

"Love is temporary at best," he said flatly.

"No." She bit her lower lip. "I won't accept that. I
know how I feel about my family. I love them with all
my heart. I would do anything for them. I gave up a
career to move back here when Frank died, yet I would
do it all again, gladly, because it was the right thing to
do."

"You gave up your career because the big city scared
you and you were happy to escape home," he told her.

But as soon as he said the words, he wanted to call
them back. Cynthia flinched. She looked as stunned as
if he'd slapped her.

"I'm sorry," he said quickly, feeling like a complete jerk. "I didn't mean that."

She didn't respond. He held out a hand to her. "Cynthia, please. Forgive me. I spoke out of turn. I know you're not like that."

Finally she reached out and took his hand in hers. "It's okay," she said. But even though she smiled, he saw the pain in her eyes.

"I'm sorry," he repeated and knew it wasn't enough.

Later that night Cynthia curled up in Jonathan's arms and listened to the sound of his steady breathing. Her body was content from their lovemaking, but her mind raced. She couldn't forget all the things they'd talked about over dinner. Worse, she couldn't convince herself that they didn't matter.

Even as he slept at her side, his words echoed in her head. That love was temporary.

He couldn't mean that, she told herself. It was so far from true. Jonathan had many faults, but ignoring the truth wasn't one of them. It was his difficult past, she told herself. The things he'd had to live with as a child. His brief outline of his relationship with his father had chilled her heart. The elder Steele had made his oldest son's life a living nightmare. Then David had grown up to hate him, turning his back on their blood relationship. In the end, Jonathan's own brother had tried to kill him. No wonder he resisted everything to do with family.

But he had to believe in love. She was convinced that in time he would come to be devoted to his nephew. They would be father and son and that would go a long way to healing Jonathan's painful wounds. As for her own feelings…she was less convinced about their future.

She desperately wanted to tell him how she felt. Tonight, while he'd spoken about his past, she'd wanted to pull him close and reassure him that everything was different now. *She* loved him, and when she loved she gave with her whole heart. Her relationship with her family was proof of that. Except...except that might not be good enough for Jonathan. He'd accused her of using her family tragedy to escape from a life that frightened her.

Cynthia disentangled herself from Jonathan and rolled onto her back. She stared up at the dark ceiling. Was that true, she asked herself. Had she used Frank's death as an opportunity to creep back home where she was safe?

Her first instinct was to dismiss Jonathan's comment. After all he'd been lashing out to protect himself. But she told herself not to be hasty. If there was even a thread of truth, she had to find it and explore what it meant. If she'd been hiding behind her family then that was a problem she needed to address. Not only for herself, but for any future she might dream of having with Jonathan and Colton.

"David's home was featured in several decorating magazines," Jonathan said as he led the way upstairs in his brother's house the next afternoon. "He had his secretary send me copies."

Behind him Cynthia sighed. "Must have been the spread under the too-white-and-scary section of the magazine," she said. "This place gives me the willies. Everything is so stark. At first I wasn't sure about your plan to sell it all and put the money in trust for Colton, but now that I'm here for the second time I know it's the right decision. Colton will be much happier growing up in your house.''

They reached the landing of the second floor. Cynthia moved next to him and smiled. He studied her face. As usual, he'd left for work before she was awake, but when he'd gone by his place to pick her up, he'd sensed that there was something wrong. That she was upset with him. He wondered if it was their conversation from the previous day. He regretted his harsh words, but aside from apologizing—which he'd already done—he didn't know how to fix the situation.

''Let's start with Colton's room,'' she said and turned in that direction.

He trailed after her. They walked into the baby's room. At his house Colton's quarters were warm and inviting. The scent of baby powder and lotion lingered in the air. There were stacks of diapers, picture books, toys and stuffed animals scattered around the room. In this elegant surrounding, there was only perfection.

Cynthia walked to the dresser and began opening drawers. ''Would you please check the closet,'' she said as she searched through stacks of tiny clothing.

''What am I looking for?''

''Anything you think Colton might want. Pictures, something old that could be a hand-me-down.''

He thought of his coolly elegant sister-in-law. ''Lisa wasn't the type.''

''Maybe not for herself, but there might be a baby quilt or blanket. Something from her family.''

He opened the closet door. There were several tiny garments on miniature hangers, along with an impossibly small coat. But nothing else. The long walk-in space was empty.

''I don't think Lisa had family,'' he said shutting the

door. "At the wedding, her side of the church had friends from college, but no relatives. Of course I was merely an invited guest, so I wouldn't have been introduced to people like that."

Cynthia glanced at him sharply. "You weren't David's best man?"

Her innocence surprised him. "I was there because David expected a big gift. The same thing happened when Colton was born, only that time I received a notice in the mail, not an invitation to the christening."

"But that's crazy."

He looked at her. "Cynthia, the man tried to have me killed."

She straightened, then sighed. "You're right. I have trouble remembering that. Mostly, I guess, because I don't want to. If I could change your past, I would. I would make everything better."

He knew she meant what she said. Because she was a dreamer who saw beauty where others only saw broken, tattered disappointments.

He found himself wanting to ease her pain, which was crazy but true. "I could have a private investigator look for Lisa's family. Maybe there are distant relatives Colton would want to meet as he got older."

His words had the desired effect. She beamed at him as if he'd caused the morning's sunrise. "I think that's great," she said.

Who was this woman who had twisted him around until he didn't know where he was or where he was going? Why did he give a damn about her feelings or opinions? And why did the sight of her happy smile make him want to take on the world?

"I'll have my secretary find research investigators in the morning," he said.

Cynthia returned her attention to the dresser drawers. "Oh, speaking of your secretary. I spoke to her this morning. She's saved some time on your schedule for the next couple of weeks so you can start interviewing potential candidates." She closed the drawer she'd gone through and moved on to the next. "She said that you would like me to be a part of the interview process."

Jonathan didn't know what to say. A different nanny living in his house? When he'd first found out he was his nephew's legal guardian, he hadn't wanted to deal with the disruption of his life. But now that Cynthia and Colton had moved in with him, he found that the disruption wasn't as bad as he thought it would be. Besides, he couldn't imagine anyone else but her caring for Colton.

She turned her head and glanced at him. "I don't mind helping," she said softly. "I do this a lot for my clients. I suggest we use my office for the interviews so that the candidates aren't in awe of their surroundings."

"Thanks," he said, when what he really wanted to ask was if she would find it easy to walk away from him. He and Cynthia shared something far beyond a working relationship. But getting involved wasn't his style. He should be pleased that she was willing to accept the time they had together for what it was and be so comfortable with moving along when they were done.

She drew a photo album from a bottom drawer and flipped through the pages. "This seems to be a record of Lisa's pregnancy. We should put this in the Keep pile."

As it was the first object they'd decided to hang on to there wasn't a pile yet, but he took the album out

into the hall to start one. From downstairs came the
sound of thumping feet.

Cynthia came out of the bedroom. "What is that?"
she asked.

"An invasion," he said cheerfully. "I called your
mother and invited her and the kids over. Not so much
to help, but to provide a distraction as we go through
the rooms. I figured ten-year-old twin boys would chase
away any ghosts."

He spoke lightly, but meant every word. He didn't
expect to ever make peace with his past. Just being in
David's house made him uncomfortable. He knew
whatever ghosts might still be in residence would wait
and follow him home so they could haunt him in the
lonely hours of darkness, moving into his dreams and
making him remember.

"We're here," Betsy called.

He and Cynthia made their way down to greet them.
The twins grinned at them.

"Mom says we can have L'Italiano deliver dinner
later, and she brought brownies for dessert," Brett said
in a rush. He turned his attention to Jonathan. "The
house is way cool. Do you have video games here?"

Betsy put one hand on each boy's shoulder. "Calm
down. Let's start with hello and a thank you to Mr.
Steele for inviting us."

"Hello," the boys chorused together.

Betsy smiled at them. "Jenny had some after-school
activities, so it's just the three of us." She looked at
Jonathan. "Are you sure you want these two terrors in
a house this beautiful. Anything breakable is at risk."

"They'll be fine," he said. He looked at the boys.
"You know, I'll bet my brother has a real high-tech

video game system. Let's go find it and you two can play.''

Brad shifted his weight from foot-to-foot. ''Can't you play with us, Mr. Steele. It'll be more fun that way.''

There was something familiar in their expression. It took him a couple of minutes to figure out that they were looking at him the same way Jenny looked at Cynthia. With complete worship.

The attention made him uncomfortable. Even so he forced himself to smile. ''Sure. I can spare the time for a couple of games.''

''Do you want me to go through the rooms and pick out my suggestions for the Keep pile?'' Cynthia asked. ''I don't mind.''

He tried not to notice that she had the same worshipful light in her eyes. ''I appreciate that,'' he told her. ''I didn't mean to leave you with all the work.''

''I'll help,'' Betsy said. ''We can indulge in girl talk. I've missed having Cynthia home these past weeks, so it will be fun.''

Jonathan knew only Betsy realized he was tarnished goods. But even she wouldn't say anything. He hated that her silence made him feel as if he should rise to everyone's expectations and be the man they wanted him to be. Didn't she know that was impossible? He did. He'd known it for years.

# Chapter 14

Cynthia sat in the middle of the living room, surrounded by boxes of pictures. "They could have put these in albums," she said, sorting the photos into piles.

Her mother had an open album in her lap. "At least this way, we can choose what goes where. What do you think, maybe three of these?" She held up photos from a cruise vacation.

"That sounds right."

At Betsy's suggestion they had collected all the loose photos they'd found in the house and were putting them together for Colton. She and her mother sat in the white-on-white living room at David's house. The floor-to-ceiling windows provided an unobstructed view of the city below. Lights twinkled in the night.

From a distance of halfway across the house came the faint sounds of beeps, crashes and laughter. She didn't know how Jonathan was surviving, but she would bet that her brothers were in ten-year-old heaven.

Speaking of brothers… Cynthia glanced at the handful of pictures she held. They were all of David as he grew up, or David with his parents, or David at school. So far she hadn't come across a single snapshot that included Jonathan. Not even the posed family portraits. It was as if he'd never existed. Brad and Brett were twins, which made them closer than most brothers. Even so she doubted there was more than one or two pictures of the boys alone. In family pictures, they were always together.

"Did you know the Steele boys went to prep school?" Betsy asked, flashing a picture of David in a school uniform.

Cynthia smiled. "I didn't know for sure, but I'm not surprised. It's the rich, you know," she said in a mock aristocratic accent. "They require a different sort of education."

"Maybe. I'm not one to speak ill of the dead, but if you ask me, David Steele looks like he didn't get enough discipline when he was growing up."

Cynthia thought about all Jonathan had told her. She considered his confidences private and hadn't shared any of them with her mother. "I suspect you're right."

They looked up as they heard footsteps on the marble floor. Jonathan walked in. He'd changed when he'd come home to get her that afternoon and wore a sweater over jeans. While she liked him wearing anything…or nothing…she had to admit that he had the kind of body made for faded denim. The fabric hugged his narrow hips and butt and made her remember how he'd looked late last night when they'd both been naked and making love.

"Okay, I know they each had a big serving of lasagna, not to mention garlic bread, less than two hours ago," he began when he entered the room. "But they're swearing that if they don't eat again, they're going to die."

Jonathan came to stop behind the white sofa across from them. He settled one hip on the back and gave Betsy an engaging grin. "I told them I would come and plead their case."

Her mother laughed. "They know I brought brownies for dessert and they're afraid I'm going to forget. Yes, they may each have one, but make them eat in the kitchen. They make a mess."

"Consider it done," he said and turned to leave. Then he faced them again. "I don't mean to sound presumptuous," he began slowly and shoved his hands into his pockets. "But there are some nice crystal and silver pieces in the hutch in the dining room and in the butler's pantry. If either of you see anything you'd like, feel free to take it. I'm not keeping any of that."

"Thank you, Jonathan," Betsy said. "I don't have much use for anything too formal, but I'll give it all a once-over before we leave. You're more than kind."

"I'd like you to take whatever you like. Or all of it." He paused, as if he was going to say more, then he left.

Cynthia returned her attention to the pictures she held. "We should go look, Mom. I'm guessing all the stuff is spectacular, even if you don't want any of it."

Her mother didn't answer. Cynthia glanced up and saw the older woman studying her. "What?" she asked.

Betsy frowned. "I'm not sure. I've just had this feeling all evening. As if there was something I didn't know. And I think I've figured it out."

Cynthia wasn't sure what her mother was talking about. "You mean because Jonathan wants us to take anything we like from the house? I know it sounds strange, but he wasn't really close to his brother.'' She pressed her lips together, wanting to be careful not to give away any secrets. ''Jonathan has had several bad family experiences. He doesn't think the way we do about heirlooms or family treasures. He's really going to sell everything and put the money in trust for Colton.''

Her mother shook her head. ''That's not what I mean,'' she said and placed the open album on the coffee table in front of her. ''You're involved with him. A few days ago you hinted that you'd fallen for him but this is more than a crush.''

It wasn't a question. Cynthia reminded herself that she was well over twenty-one and that she hadn't done anything wrong. Even so she felt herself blushing. ''I don't know that I'd call it involved. We're...'' Her voice trailed off, then she decided she might as well tell the truth.

''I love him,'' she said. ''I don't think he loves me back, but we're friends and he cares about me.''

Her mother blinked. ''I'll admit I'd expected a lot of things, but not that. Love. Are you sure?''

She wished she weren't. Loving Jonathan wasn't easy. He was a sophisticated man who traveled in circles she'd never been a part of.

''As sure as I can be. He's everything I've ever wanted in a man. I know he's not perfect, but who is? I admire many things about him.'' She frowned. ''It's not about money or power, Mom. I swear. If anything, that stuff makes me nervous.''

Her mother dismissed the comment with a wave. ''I know that. You weren't raised to find those things important. Of course no one wants to be homeless, but once the basic needs are met, finances don't enter into it.''

Her mother leaned back into the sofa and sighed. ''But Jonathan Steele. I don't know. He's so...not like us. He's an emotionally closed man. If you can be the one to open him up, if he comes to truly trust you, then I believe he'll be a good and faithful partner. But I don't know that anyone has the power to reach him.'' She fixed her gaze on her daughter. ''I don't want to see you get hurt.''

''I don't want that, either,'' Cynthia agreed, knowing it was a very real possibility. ''Unfortunately it's a little late to be worrying about that. I'm sort of up to my neck already.'' She set down the pictures she'd been holding and sighed. ''It's not just Jonathan, either. It's Colton. I know better than to get emotionally involved with one of the babies, but I have to admit he's stolen my heart.''

She looked at her mother. ''Just to make my life interesting, we're supposed to start interviewing permanent nannies soon. I got a call from his secretary this morning arranging our schedules so we could coordinate everything. I wanted to scream at her that losing Colton would hurt too much, but I can't. I have to be a professional.''

The pain from that conversation returned. ''I don't know what to do,'' she admitted in a quiet voice. ''I'm not sure how to survive losing them both.''

Her mother slid toward her and gathered her close. ''I know. I wish I could say or do something to make it better, but I can't. You're going to have to see this to the end.'' She touched Cynthia's face. ''However this turns out, you know I'm here for you, don't you?''

Cynthia nodded. She knew she was too old to need

her mother's approval or embrace to make her feel better, but she couldn't deny the comfort the hug brought her.

Betsy slid back to her side of the sofa. "It might all work out," she said. "You can't be sure yet. And if it doesn't, you'll get through what you have to. I've learned that lesson myself."

Cynthia thought about all her mother had been through—being thrown out by her parents when she was only eighteen and the mother of a three-year-old, the loss of her husband—and knew that having her relationship with Jonathan fail wasn't even close.

"You're right, of course," she said, feeling slightly ashamed. "I couldn't miss Jonathan as much as you have missed Frank."

"Why not?" her mother asked. Betsy smiled sadly. "If you love him as much as I loved Frank, then you'll miss him as much. I wish you wouldn't, but those kinds of feelings don't die easily."

Returning footsteps interrupted them. Cynthia forced herself to smile pleasantly at Jonathan so he wouldn't suspect that they'd been talking about anything important. Fortunately he didn't seem to notice the charged atmosphere in the room.

He stood behind the sofa across from them and shifted his weight from foot to foot. "Here's the thing," he said. "I was wondering if there was a reason the boys didn't have a video-game player at home. I mean do you think it's a bad thing, that it will keep them from their homework or playing outside?"

He swallowed and avoided both their gazes. "It's just that they're really having a good time and I'm getting rid of it anyway and I thought maybe if you didn't mind, they could take it home with them. It has a really nice carrying case and lots of games. Oh, and a Mute button.''

Betsy laughed. She tucked her short blond curls behind her ears. ''I don't have any moral opposition to video games,'' she said. ''Brad and Brett aren't the type of kids to sit in front of the television all day. They have too much energy. You're very kind and we appreciate that.''

He grinned. ''Great. Can I tell them? Or do you want to?''

''Go ahead.''

''Thanks.'' He turned on his heel and left the room.

Betsy gazed after him and sighed. ''They already look up to him,'' she said. ''This is going to give him God-like stature in their eyes. I can't decide if that's good or bad.''

Cynthia was pleased that Jonathan seemed to be getting along so well with her brothers. ''He's a terrific role model for them. He's honest and smart and he'll never lead them astray. I know he's not Frank, Mom, but no one would be.''

Betsy didn't look convinced. ''You're seeing him through love's eyes. That gives everyone a glow. I'm not so convinced. Of course if he breaks your heart, I'll have to hate him on general principle.''

Cynthia appreciated that her mother was worried about her, but she didn't think it was going to help. Either she and Jonathan could work things out or they couldn't. ''I believe in him,'' she said firmly, but as she spoke the words she wasn't sure if she was convincing her mother, or herself.

Jonathan glanced in his rearview mirror. ''You all right back there?''

There wasn't a reply. Not a big surprise, he told himself. After all, Colton's verbal abilities barely stretched to gurgling. Still the baby waved his arms in excitement, as if the thought of being in Jonathan's car was a treat beyond measure.

"Just wait a few years until you're big enough to sit in the front seat," he said. "That'll be even better."

Colton grinned, then turned away as a large truck caught his attention. He pointed and made his favorite raspberry sound. Jonathan turned right at the corner and pulled into the parking lot.

Jonathan found himself driving more slowly than usual as he maneuvered through the maze of cars, just as he'd been extra careful on the twenty-minute drive from his house to Cynthia's office. He'd always considered himself an excellent driver, but having a baby in the back seat had made him more cautious than usual.

"Next thing you know I'll have one of those stupid Baby On Board stickers on the back window," he muttered to himself as he turned off the ignition and got out of the car. He could only imagine the expression on his Mercedes dealer's face when he drove in for his yearly service. Jonathan Steele, a father? Not likely.

"That's why we're getting you a nanny," he told Colton when he opened the back door and reached in to unfasten the infant from his car seat. "We're going to find a nice lady to come live in the house and take care of you. Like Cynthia has been, but this will be a more permanent arrangement. Sort of a mom for hire."

Colton seemed more interested in the pen in his jacket pocket than by the conversation. Jonathan pulled the writing instrument from harm's way, then tucked the baby securely in his arms. "It's up here," he said, walking toward the four-storey building.

Mother's Helper had a good-size office suite on the third floor of the building. He entered the reception area. A young woman behind a counter looked up and smiled.

"You must be Mr. Steele. Cynthia is expecting you. If you'll follow me?"

Jonathan glanced at the five women seated in the waiting area. They were probably the candidates for the job. None of them especially appealed to him, but then he reminded himself that good looks weren't important. What he wanted was a trained professional who would provide consistent, loving care for his nephew. Still there weren't even any warm grandmother-types. Just four straight-backed older women in dark dresses and a younger woman who barely looked out of her teens. She caught Jonathan's glance and smiled welcomingly. His brain screamed trouble.

He followed the receptionist down a carpeted hall. The office décor was understated and elegant, done in various shades of green. At the end of the hall the receptionist paused, knocked on a closed door, then pushed it open to admit him.

Jonathan stepped into Cynthia's office. He hadn't known what to expect. The large room had a view of the rear parking lot and several trees. There was a fabric-covered sofa to the left, three bookcases and a big L-shaped desk in front of the window. Cynthia sat behind the latter. She scribbled something on a pad of paper while she talked on the telephone. She glanced up briefly, smiled at both him and Colton, then returned her attention to the call.

"I'm afraid I have to go now, Mrs. Beech, but someone from the office will be in touch by the end of the day.'' She listened. "Yes. I understand completely. Goodbye.''

As she hung up, she rose to her feet. "Hi. How are my two favorite guys?''

Before Jonathan could speak, Colton caught sight of her. Or maybe it had been the sound of her voice. Either way the baby went crazy, cooing and wriggling and holding out his arms in obvious delight.

Cynthia came around the desk and took Colton from him. "Goodness. I've only been gone a few hours. Did you really miss me that much?''

Apparently Colton had because he giggled as soon as Cynthia cuddled him close. She kissed the top of his head, then looked at Jonathan. "You found your way here all right?''

"Sure. It was easy.'' He glanced around her office, then motioned at the framed McKnight prints on her walls. "Very nice.''

She laughed and led the way to her sofa. "I doubt that it comes close to anything in your office, but it works for me.'' She set Colton on her lap. "I'm sure you noticed the candidates in the waiting area. There are five altogether. Today's interviews are preliminary. Our goal is to try to weed out the ones that aren't going to work and to get to know the 'possibles.'''

She continued to talk about interview questions and technique, but he wasn't listening. He found his attention captured by the way Colton relaxed in her arms and gazed up at her with adoration.

"How is he going to react to all this?'' he asked, interrupting her and pointing at the baby. "Hasn't he already had too many changes in his life?''

Cynthia glanced down at his nephew and smiled. Her

expression softened and her gaze took on a loving, maternal look he'd never noticed before.

"Colton is a sweetheart," she said. "He's had a lot of traumas in his life, but he's basically a happy, affectionate child. That means he'll probably accept the new nanny easily and that she'd quickly adore him. There is always a time of transition. The way we handle it here is that the temporary nanny continues to spend time with the baby during a transitionary period, easing in the permanent caregiver. I thought that's how you and I would handle this. That is if you don't object."

"Sounds like you've thought of everything," he said truthfully.

She grinned. "Hey, that's part of my job."

In these surroundings, Cynthia was in charge. This was her business, her turf. Although he'd known in his head that she owned a company, he'd never thought about her in those terms. In his mind she'd been the too-young woman who had invaded his life and tempted him beyond reason. But she was much more than that. How come he'd never noticed before?

"I didn't mean to keep you from your work," he said. "You've been trapped in my house for several weeks when you should have been here."

"I've come in a few times," she said. "I'll admit that I take less in-home assignments now than I did when I was just starting, which is too bad. I really enjoy working with the babies. So this has been a lot of fun for me. Please don't worry that my company has suffered. I have an excellent staff who have kept things running smoothly." She glanced at her watch. "Speaking of which, are you ready to start the interviews?"

He nodded, even though he hated the idea of speaking to all those people about his nephew. He didn't want anyone in his house but Cynthia. However that wasn't an option. Obviously Cynthia wasn't broken up about leaving his employ, so why should he think he'd miss *her?* He could play the game as well as anyone. In fact, he could play it better.

The last candidate stepped out of the office and closed the door behind her. Cynthia leaned back in her seat and sighed. She felt as if she'd run a marathon. "That's the last of them," she said.

"I would say we have two serious possibilities," Jonathan said, staring at his pad of notes. "I hadn't thought we'd get so far on the first round, but I'm impressed by the people you brought me and their qualifications."

Cynthia nodded with an enthusiasm she didn't feel. Any one of the six nannies would have been fine. As Jonathan said, two of them had been excellent matches. Between their qualifications and their immediate rapport with Colton, they were obvious front-runners. Which should have made her very happy. After all, that meant her work at the Steele house was nearly complete. She could start thinking about getting back to her own life.

Except nothing about this afternoon felt right. She hated the thought of someone else living in her room, taking care of Colton and being with Jonathan. Intellectually she knew that he wasn't going to start an affair with the new nanny. The fact that the two he liked best were at least fifteen years older than he was the least of it. He didn't go around preying on the hired help. Their relationship was a quirk of fate or something. But she hated the thought that she was so very replaceable.

"What's wrong?" he asked.

She shook her head even as she had the silliest urge to burst into tears. Over the past week or so she'd spent a lot of time searching her heart to define her feelings about Jonathan. She accepted that she loved him, but she'd wanted to explore his accusation that she'd been willing to leave her career in Chicago to come home because she was afraid.

What she'd decided was he was wrong. She'd enjoyed her job and her life in the city. When her mother had needed her, she'd come back without a second thought because it was the right thing to do and because she wanted to be close to her family. But none of it had been about running away.

She'd also realized that her feelings for Jonathan weren't a simple crush. Her love was real and deep and it wasn't going to fade anytime soon. Which didn't change the fact that he had other plans for them. He seemed almost happy to be replacing her.

"Cynthia, what is it?" he asked, leaning forward on the sofa. She sat in her desk chair, which she'd pulled around to face the sofa.

She started to deny anything was wrong, then changed her mind. She stared at him, taking in the tailored suit and handsome features. At one time he'd been an imposing stranger, but now he was as dear to her as anyone else she loved.

"How can you let me go?" she asked softly.

He frowned. "I don't understand. We always knew your employment was temporary. I'm a little concerned about Colton's adjustment, but I think we can make that work."

He was being completely professional...and ripping her heart out at the same time.

"I'm not talking about Colton. I'm referring to us. Our relationship. Once you have a new nanny, I'll be moving out. Is that a natural breaking point for you?"

She was able to keep her voice calm and steady, despite the tightness in her throat. She didn't want to show weakness in front of him and she certainly didn't want to cry.

He leaned back into the sofa. "I don't know," he said simply. "What do you think should happen?"

She hadn't realized how much she'd been hoping for until it wasn't there. She shivered as if the temperature in her office had dropped fifty degrees.

"I thought I mattered," she murmured, unable to look at him. She studied the hem of her dress as if it was the most interesting thing in the room. The dark wool was smooth and perfectly pressed. "I thought—" She had to clear her throat to go on. "I fell in love with you, Jonathan."

She looked up in time to see him flinch as if she'd struck him. He swore. "Don't say that. I don't want you to love me."

She gave a harsh laugh that had nothing to do with humor and everything to do with pain. "That's right. You wanted to have sex with me, but you don't want to care about me."

He rose to his feet and glared at her. "It's not like that and you know it."

"Then what is it like?"

He ran his fingers through his hair, then turned and crossed to the window. "Dammit, Cynthia, don't care about me. I've told you before, I'm not worth it. I'll only hurt you."

"You *are* hurting me, but that doesn't change the truth."

He spun to face her. "I don't want this truth."

She couldn't stop the tears that sprang to her eyes.

Pain filled her, a sharp, breath-stealing pain that made her feel as if she were being turned inside out.

"I can't give you whatever it is you think you want," he continued.

"Why do I have to want something?"

"Everyone does. You wouldn't be telling me this if you didn't have an expectation. What is it? Marriage? You want the name and money?"

His cold, ugly words tore at her like wild dogs. She felt bits of herself being flung around the room. Worse, he was right. She *did* have expectations and wants. Until that moment she hadn't realized that by loving him, she'd allowed herself to believe in the fantasy. That they would be together forever. Her, Jonathan and Colton. She'd imagined the children they would have together. A family of her own.

But he wouldn't want to hear that from her. Already he looked panicked, as if the door was too far away and he couldn't wait to be gone.

"I thought we had something special," she said. "I'm sorry that my loving you is so uncomfortable."

"There is no love," he growled. "It's a convenient thing to say when people are trying to manipulate each other. My mother and father were supposed to be in love and look what happened there. She didn't have any trouble falling in love with someone else and running off. My own brother should have loved me, but he tried to kill me, instead. There is no love. Just excuses."

He radiated anger and pain. A different kind from her own, but very real. She looked at the face that had become so familiar to her. At the shape of his mouth and the color of his eyes. She knew his body well enough to find him blindfolded, guided by scent alone. She knew how to please him in bed, how to make him laugh.

She didn't understand the complexities of his world, but they were becoming clearer all the time. She thought she'd earned his trust and had perhaps claimed a small piece of his heart, but she'd only been fooling herself.

The truth was, she'd lost him...assuming she'd ever had him at all.

She rose to her feet. "I can't agree with anything you're saying about love," she told him. "I know you've had some horrible things happen in your past. I also know it doesn't have to be like that. I am familiar with the workings of my heart, and I do love you with a strength that can't be explained away. I apologize for any discomfort my feelings have caused you. That was never my intent. I had h-hoped—"

For the first time her voice faltered.

"I had hoped it would be different," she managed to say after taking a deep breath. "But even if this is how it ends, I won't regret loving you. Not for a minute."

Jonathan had his back against the wall and there was nowhere to go. If they hadn't been on the third floor he would have considered climbing out the window and escaping that way.

He couldn't bear to be in the same room with her. Everything she said hit him below the belt, landing on his gut like a sucker punch. He felt as if he'd been run over by a train. He had to make her stop talking.

"Despite everything," she said with a smile that didn't come close to reaching her eyes. "I still think you're a wonderful man."

Her inherent belief, in spite of all he'd said, nearly drove him to his knees. Didn't she realize that he'd survived all the crap in his life by learning to stand on his own? He didn't need anyone else, and that solitary existence had kept him safe. But now she wanted to change the rules. She wanted to invite herself into his world, his life, his very being and expose him. Once she got what she wanted, she would have all the power. If he needed her, then she could leave. If he let himself believe she loved him, then she could destroy him by taking that love away.

Because she wasn't telling the truth. She did want something from him. She wanted him to love her back. She wanted him to be so desperately in love with her that he would offer her his heart and soul.

What she didn't know, and he would make sure she never knew, was that with her, he'd allowed himself to see the possibilities. The "what if" of the future had touched him with warmth and light. But he knew better than to believe. His cold, empty world was a safe place from which to operate.

"Whatever you take away from this," she said quietly. "I want you to know that you've been an amazing part of my life. You are everything I thought you'd be. Good and kind, intelligent and patient. You will be a terrific father to Colton."

He stared at her. She wore a pale blouse tucked into a wool skirt. With her hair pinned up, she looked professional and capable. Not the innocent he knew her to be. He had to get rid of her before she convinced him it was safe to try. He knew the cost of losing love. He'd learned that lesson when he lost both parents within hours of each other. His mother had walked away without giving him a second glance and his father had turned his back on him as punishment for being his mother's son. David's attitude had only reinforced the lesson.

Cynthia was nothing but a dangerous fool.

"You can't love me," he said coldly. "Because you

don't know the first thing about me. I'm a lowlife bastard. You should have learned that a long time ago.''
He walked toward her and stared directly into her face.

"I want you out of my house today," he said clearly.
"I'll expect all traces of you gone by the time I return
from work. You will provide me with a suitable replacement. In return I will decide on a permanent nanny for
Colton by the end of the week."

## *Chapter 15*

There was an old saying about being careful what one wished for. After all, it might come true. Jonathan considered the ancient truth that night as he sat alone in his study. He sipped the brandy he cradled, but the fiery liquid couldn't erase the sense of emptiness inside of him.

The house was as he liked it—quiet, cold. He should have felt perfectly at home, but he didn't. He felt as if he'd just lost his entire world and nothing was ever going to be right again.

Which was ridiculous, he told himself. There was a new nanny in residence. Mrs. Miller seemed well-qualified and competent. She'd told him earlier that she was a widow with seven grandchildren. She took short-term temporary assignments to give her pin money and to get her out of the house. Her harmless chatter had helped him pretend that everything was fine. The charade had lasted until both Colton and the eminently experienced Mrs. Miller were down for the night. It was only then the ghosts had appeared.

His usual specters were oddly quiet. Instead he found himself haunted by memories of a young woman who had somehow made a place for herself in his supposedly closed and unscalable world. What should have been a night of peace had instead become one of pain and aching aloneness.

The sound of her footsteps seemed to fill the silence. He would swear he could hear the echo of her laughter and inhale the sweet scent of her body. As he held the brandy snifter, he thought he felt warm flesh instead of cool glass. She had done as he'd asked and disappeared from his world, and yet he felt her presence more strongly than ever.

Jonathan closed his eyes and told himself that everything would be fine now. He had all that he wanted. He was once more responsible only for himself.

But he wasn't. Upstairs a small child slept. His nephew. With David and Lisa's deaths he'd become guardian to an innocent baby. From now until he drew in his last breath, he would have to worry and plan for a world that included Colton Steele.

The thought confounded him. A child. A baby. Soon that baby would begin to walk and talk. He would grow and attend school. Jonathan would have to help him with his reading and play sports with him. There would be school conferences and family vacations. In time he and Colton would discuss girls, sex and careers. He would teach the boy to drive.

Jonathan opened his eyes and stared into the darkness. He couldn't imagine that any of it was real. Him, a father? He didn't know how. All he knew was the abandonment of his parents and a life of isolation. He didn't know where to begin to change that for Colton. Cynthia said that what Colton needed the most was love and Jonathan didn't know how to do that.

He'd always told himself that families were an invention of the devil and he hadn't changed his mind. No doubt Lucifer himself was having a good laugh at his expense right about now. Jonathan drew in a deep breath and leaned his head against the back of the chair. He'd never felt more alone in his life. He ached for her.

And yet he would find a way to go on without her because he couldn't be the things she needed him to be. Because he didn't know how to love her and he wouldn't offer her less than she deserved. No, he thought grimly. All that was bull. He'd never been selfless enough to give a damn about anyone else. The real reason he wouldn't have her in his world was that he couldn't risk caring about her and having her leave. Once he allowed himself to love Cynthia, he wouldn't survive her going away. Because everyone left eventually. They always had.

Cynthia sat curled up in the lone chair in her bedroom. The cramped quarters—filled with a full-size bed, a small desk and low bookcase—had been her haven for over ten years. She loved this room. All through high school and beyond, it had been her refuge. Yet now it could have been a hotel room for all the comfort it gave.

She glanced at the clock. It was nearly nine in the evening. She hadn't eaten, but she wasn't hungry. She doubted she would be able to sleep later, either. She felt as if she'd been run over and left as roadkill. It hurt to think and breathe and even to stay upright in the chair.

If this was love, she'd made a big mistake giving in to it so easily.

A knock on the door forced her to gather her waning strength enough to speak. "Come in," she called.

Jenny entered, carrying a tray with a pot of tea, two cups and a plate of cookies. "Mom says it's okay not to eat anything, but you have to drink the tea. The cookies are my idea. They always make me feel better."

Jenny's thirteen-year-old features were so earnest and caring, Cynthia couldn't help smiling. "Thanks. I'm doing okay."

Jenny set the tray on the desk, then poured them each a cup of tea. She took hers to the bed and settled cross-legged in the center of the mattress. "You don't look okay and you don't act okay. Plus I can tell when you're lying. Mom says that's a good thing. That we're all lousy liars, I mean." She offered a quick smile that faded almost as soon as it began. "I'm sorry about what happened with Mr. Steele."

Cynthia reached for her tea and took a sip of the steaming liquid. "Me, too. I guess it's going to take some time to get over him."

Her sister, a younger version of their mother, tilted her head. "I don't understand. I know Mr. Steele liked you a lot. I could see it when he looked at you."

Surprisingly Jenny's comment eased the band of pressure around her chest. "Thank you for saying that. But liking isn't the same as loving. I love him and that's not what he wants from me." She paused and stared into the mug, as if the answers to her questions awaited at the bottom among the few floating tea leaves. "But it's more than that. I have expectations that he doesn't think he can fulfill."

"Like what?"

Cynthia shrugged. "Jonathan didn't have the same kind of home that we did."

"Yeah, his was bigger."

Cynthia actually smiled. The tugging of her mouth into a grin felt awkward, but also good. "Agreed, but I don't mean that. His parents weren't like ours. His mother ran off when he was only five and his father ignored him. He was alone in that big house with no one to love him. Because of that he's afraid to believe that I love him."

"He'll change his mind," her sister said with the confidence of youth. "Now that you're gone, he'll miss you a lot and come after you."

"I would like that very much, but I have my doubts." She looked at her sister. "Either way, I have a business and a life." She paused. "Jenny, it's time for me to move out. Mom is doing much better and I need to be on my own."

Jenny clutched the mug she held and pressed her lips tightly together. Tears filled her eyes. "I know," she whispered. "Mom already told me. She said that you'd given up too much already by living with us and that you needed a chance to live by yourself." She sniffed. "But I can still come visit, can't I?"

"Absolutely. I kinda hoped you'd spend the night with me once in a while. So we can have some girl time together."

Jenny smiled bravely. "I'd like that. I just wish you didn't have to go."

"I know." But Cynthia knew that being on her own would force her to get on with her life. Her hope was that then she would find things to distract her from thoughts of Jonathan. She needed to get on with the business of healing or she would spend the rest of her life wishing for something that was never going to happen.

"Mr. Jonathan, it's the baby," Lucinda said, her voice agitated.

Jonathan clutched the receiver as panic filled him. "What happened?"

"Nothing. The little one won't eat. Mrs. Miller, she tried everything, but he only looks at her and turns his head. I don't think he's sick. I think he misses Miss Cynthia. I tried to give him a bottle, but he won't take it for me, either. He has before, but not now. Mr. Jonathan, you have to come home right away. If he won't eat for you, then we have to take him to the doctor."

It was the middle of the workday and he had a full calendar. His meetings ran until eight-thirty that evening. "I'll be right there," he said and hung up. Then he buzzed his secretary and informed her that he needed to reschedule everything.

He arrived home less than twenty minutes after Lucinda's call and jogged into the house. His housekeeper stood at the bottom of the stairs, wringing her hands in her apron.

"Oh, Mr. Jonathan, it's so sad. He just looks at me with those big eyes. I think there have been too many changes in his life. It's not good for the baby." Her expression turned accusing. "You should have kept Miss Cynthia longer."

"I don't doubt you're right," he said, taking the stairs two at a time.

He entered the baby's room and found Mrs. Miller pacing with Colton in her arms. She turned and gave him an apologetic smile. "I'm sorry to bother you, sir.

I don't usually have a problem getting babies to eat for me, but this little lad is stubborn.''

"It runs in the family," Jonathan said. "You don't think he's ill?''

"No. Just not himself. Although if he won't eat for you, then I would recommend we get him to the pediatrician right away.''

Jonathan didn't tell the concerned nanny that he'd never once fed Colton and did not have a clue as to how to do it. But the baby had smiled at him when he entered the room and now held out his arms.

Jonathan walked over to Mrs. Miller and carefully took Colton from his arms. The infant cooed, then relaxed.

"Here." The nanny handed him a bottle. "See if he'll take it.''

But there wasn't a doubt. Colton saw the incoming meal and squealed. He latched onto the nipple firmly and sucked with all his baby might.

"He was hungry," Mrs. Miller said. "I'm not surprised. He hasn't eaten since early last evening." She walked toward the hall. "I'll just leave you two to finish things up." And then she was gone.

Jonathan walked over to the rocker in the corner and carefully sat down. He'd held Colton enough not to feel completely awkward about having the baby in his arms. As for the feeding part, he guessed Colton would drink until he was full. He had a vague thought that after the eating there was a burping ritual, but Mrs. Miller could explain that to him. For now it was enough to watch his nephew suck happily.

"You miss her," Jonathan murmured. "Hell, I miss her, too, but at least I have sense enough to eat.''

Blue eyes regarded him thoughtfully.

"I know what you're thinking," Jonathan said. "If you won't take a bottle from Mrs. Miller, what's going to happen with the issue of solid food? Cynthia said you had to start that pretty soon. I don't know the first thing about babies, you know. Plus, I have a company to run. I can't spend all day with you. So we have a really big problem."

The sucking had grown less frantic. He looked down and saw that Colton had closed one baby fist around the lapel of his jacket and was holding on tight.

Something warm flared to life inside his chest. Something that grew and spread until the heat filled him with an inner peace. At the same time, he felt a fierce protectiveness toward this small life. Colton had no one in the world but him. He, too, was alone. So maybe together they had a chance to matter to each other. After all, they were family.

"I don't know the first thing about being a father," Jonathan warned him. "But then I'm guessing your standards aren't too high. Maybe we can figure it out together."

He looked at David's only son. A child of the brother who had stolen from him and tried to have him killed. It was time to put all that behind him, he realized. If he'd really hated his brother, he would have had David arrested months ago, instead of giving him time to change his mind and even, at the last minute, a chance to put the money back. As much as they hadn't known what to do with the relationship, he and David had been family as well.

Then, for the first time, he bent down and kissed Colton's forehead. Despite the bottle in his mouth, the baby smiled. Jonathan knew that he was a goner and there wasn't a damn thing he could do about it. Worse, he found he didn't want to do anything.

If this was love, it actually wasn't so bad.

A pounding on the front door interrupted Jonathan's concentration. It was late in the afternoon. Under normal circumstances he would have been at the office, but since Colton had become stubborn about eating only for him, he'd started working out of the house.

He had a brief, unrealistic thought that it was Cynthia, then told himself to stop being a fool. He returned his attention to his computer, only to be interrupted by Lucinda.

She stuck her head inside the study. "You have visitors." She hesitated. "It's Jenny and the boys, but Miss Cynthia isn't with them."

Her faintly accusing gaze told him that she still hadn't forgiven him for allowing Cynthia to leave. Lucinda didn't know the details of their argument, but she didn't much care. Whatever happened had to have been his fault and in her mind, it was up to him to fix it.

He rose and went to greet the children. Until he actually saw them standing in the center of the foyer, he hadn't realized how much he'd been hoping that Lucinda was wrong—that the woman who had haunted his dreams really had accompanied them. But the three kids stood in a tight group, balanced on their in-line skates, not smiling, barely glancing up when he walked over and greeted them.

"How's it going?" he asked brightly. "Jenny, you look great. Brad, Brett, how's school?"

Brad, the usually silent twin, slid off his backpack and opened it. "Here," he said, dumping a video game player onto the marble floor. Brett did the same, upending a dozen games. The plastic cases skidded across the slick floor. Both boys straightened.

"We don't want the game," Brad said fiercely, his blue eyes bright with unshed tears. "That's what we came to tell you."

"Yeah. You were mean to our sister. You made Cynthia cry." Brett's voice was defiant, as if he knew he wasn't allowed to talk to adults like that but refused to care this time.

Jenny put her arms around both boys. "We don't know what happened, Mr. Steele, but Cynthia is very hurt right now. The three of us decided it would be best to return the game." Looking so much like her beautiful older sister, she raised her chin. "We won't be seeing you again."

He hadn't thought that three children could have the power to wound him so deeply, but as he felt the blows their words delivered, he knew they could cut him down to his soul. He hadn't realized their good opinion mattered, but it did, and now it was lost.

What was he supposed to say? How could he explain something that didn't quite make sense to him? "I'm sorry," he said, haltingly. "I never wanted to—"

"Don't apologize."

Everyone turned toward the open front door. Cynthia stood there. She ignored Jonathan in favor of her siblings. "I can't believe you three did this. It's very rude and it's wrong. I want you to go home now, but don't think it's over. We'll be talking later."

The children gave him one last condemning look before skating out of the house. When they were gone, Cynthia closed the door behind them and glanced at him.

"Sorry about that," she said, her voice carefully

light. "I didn't realize what they had planned until it was too late to stop them. When I figured it out, I drove right over. I'd hoped I could intercept them, but kids on in-line skates can really move."

He couldn't breathe. The sight of her should have been like water to a man dying in the desert, but he couldn't believe she was really here. All the pain, the emptiness and loneliness crashed in on him. He hadn't known what she'd meant to him until he'd lost her and now she was back...but not for long. Not forever.

But he didn't want forever. He wanted—

Except Jonathan Steele, maker of billions of dollars, didn't know what he wanted. Or what was important. Or what it would take to figure out how to keep Cynthia when he knew that what she needed was love and he didn't think he knew how.

"They don't understand," she was saying. "They're not used to seeing me upset, which I confess I have been. It hurt them and they lashed out. They're too young to understand that you're the wronged party, not me. You never asked me to fall in love with you or hinted that our relationship would be anything but professional." She offered a sad smile. "I'm the one who crossed the line, not you."

She was dressed in her usual uniform of jeans and a sweatshirt. Her hair was back in a ponytail, her face free of makeup. She wasn't elegant or sophisticated, but she was the most beautiful woman he'd ever seen.

"I understand how that could have happened," he said. "You didn't have much experience in my world."

This time her smile was genuine. "You're right about that. And I'll admit that I did have dreams about a future. Marriage, more children." She shrugged. "Just call me Cinderella. Isn't that what you said when we met?''

He didn't remember, but then he couldn't think. Not about anything but what she said. Marriage, more children. Is that what she wanted? With him? Would she really trust him that much? Enough to let him marry her and father her children?

But he wasn't good enough. He didn't know how. Couldn't she see the dark places inside of him? He'd been the one to say that families were an invention of the devil. While he no longer believed that, she couldn't know about his change.

"How is Colton?" she asked.

He focused on her question and ignored everything else. "He hasn't been doing well. That's why I'm home. I've spoken with the pediatrician and she says it's all the changes in his life."

Cynthia's expression tightened as color fled her face. "What's wrong? Is he ill?"

"No. He hasn't taken to Mrs. Miller. I have to feed him, which I don't mind, but he's a little restless with her. The doctor says it's the lack of stability in his situation."

Cynthia took a step toward him. "I don't mind coming back. I promise I won't say or do anything inappropriate. But if it would be easier until you've chosen a permanent nanny, I'm happy to fill in."

He didn't know how to answer that. He knew that he'd hurt her terribly and yet she was willing to be around him for the sake of the baby. If she were any other woman, he would suspect her of trying to use the situation to her advantage, but that wasn't Cynthia's style. He might be a jerk, but he wasn't stupid. He'd learned his lesson about her.

"Why don't you come see him now," he said, motioning to the stairs.

She gave him a grateful smile, then hurried toward the second floor.

Ten minutes later she sat in the rocking chair in the baby's bedroom. Colton had screamed with delight when he saw her and was just beginning to stop wiggling with pleasure as she held him.

Jonathan stood in the doorway, watching the two of them together. He saw the light in Cynthia's eyes—the same light she had when she looked at Jenny or the boys. The same light Betsy had when she looked at her children. The glow came from a mother's love. At one time the realization would have terrified him, but now he knew it wouldn't go out—that Cynthia's feelings would last for the rest of her life.

He dropped his gaze to Colton. The baby was as innocent of his father's crimes as Jonathan had been of his mother's. He saw that now. His father had been wrong to blame him, just as he, Jonathan, would be wrong to blame Colton. Not that he planned to do any such thing.

"I love him," he said quietly.

Cynthia looked up and smiled. "I hoped you would. Loving a child is the most pure act we humans are capable of. Especially loving a child who isn't our own. It's a selfless giving that returns the most amazing reward. For being loved by that child is the greatest gift of all."

He looked at her and knew that he'd been a fool to ever let her go. She was the best part of his world. She who gave from the very depths of her being, had offered him her heart and he'd turned it down. Because he'd been afraid and unworthy. He might never be worthy, but he could stop being a coward.

"I don't agree with you," he told her. "I think the greatest gift is to be loved by someone who sees only the best in other people. Someone good and kind, yet smart and fun to be with."

Cynthia stared at him. He could tell that she didn't know what to think about his words.

"If you thought walking away from me was the best for me, not for you," he said, "would you do it?"

She frowned. "Of course."

He took a step toward her. "You'll always be the better person. Because I know that the best thing for me is to walk away from you and there's no way in hell I'm going to let you go." He took another step, then shoved his hands into his jeans pockets.

"I'm standing at the crossroads of my life," he said. "My heart and my soul ache. One of the paths in front of me leads to the autonomy and loneliness I've always known. You and Colton are the other path. He's stuck with me, but you get to make a choice."

He paused and found he was nervous. He had to clear his throat before speaking. "If you were someone else, I would try to seduce you with my net worth, but if you were that person I wouldn't be interested, so what's the point?"

Her hazel-green eyes were huge in her still face, but she didn't speak. He kind of hoped she would at least give him a hint as to what she was thinking, but when she didn't, he was forced to go on.

"I don't have anything to offer you," he said haltingly. "Nothing really important. I don't know how to love you or be a good husband. I only know that if you give me another chance, you won't regret it. I'll learn how to be the man you deserve. I'll show you in a thousand different ways how important you are to me, how amazing it is that I can finally understand what it means to love someone.''

She shifted Colton so that she could hold out one of her hands. She rose to her feet and covered the last step that separated them. ''You don't have to do any of that,'' she whispered as tears filled her eyes and she touched his arm. ''All you have to do is trust me enough to let me love you and try to love me back. Time will take care of the rest.''

He wasn't sure who reached for whom, but suddenly they were embracing, careful of the happy baby between them. Jonathan touched her and kissed her and stroked her face.

''I love you,'' he said. ''Both of you. And your family. I want you in my life. All of you. I can't let you go. I want you to be Colton's mother and my wife and I want to give you as many babies as you want. Just promise you'll never leave.'' He cupped her face in his hands. ''You are my world, Cynthia. I couldn't survive without you.''

She continued to cry, but he had grown enough to recognize happy tears when he saw them. ''Tell me you'll marry me,'' he said.

She laughed. ''In a hot minute. I love you. I want to be with you for always.'' She pressed her mouth to his. ''Oh, and this is where I point out that I've always known you were a good and loving man. You've fought me on that point, but I was right.''

Some of the tension inside of him eased. She was his. He wasn't going to have to learn to live without her. Love. Did he really feel it? He searched his full heart and knew that it had been there all along...waiting to be let out.

"Whatever I am, it's because of you," he told her.

They kissed again. As he held her Jonathan knew that there was much work yet to be done. He had to make things right with Jenny and the boys. He had to talk to Betsy and convince her that he was good enough for her oldest daughter. Then he had to take Cynthia to bed and make love with her until they were both breathless. Finally there was a wedding to plan.

But he faced the future with a sense of joy and hope he'd never felt before. With Cynthia at his side, he knew he could do anything...even give his heart for a lifetime.

\* \* \* \* \*

# Chapter 1

"I need help here, White!"

The bark of the doctor's voice cut through the din of the emergency room and nurse Tina White looked up from the patient she was bandaging. "I'll be right there," she called.

She looked down at the woman lying on the table with an encouraging smile. "You're going to be fine," she said, her voice low and reassuring.

Giving the woman another reassuring smile, Tina moved to the next cubicle. The emergency room doctor was working on an unconscious man, and Tina moved to the other side of the exam table. Her stomach clenched as she looked at the blood that covered his face and the left side of his head. "Surely he didn't get these injuries in the chaos at the masquerade ball?" she asked, moving instinctively to staunch the flow of blood from the man's head.

"Car accident," the doctor answered tersely as he

examined the patient. "The police said he was chasing the guy who killed the Steeles at the ball."

Tina raised her head and looked over at the doctor. "You mean he was trying to catch the killer?"

The doctor shrugged. "Maybe he was the guy's accomplice. We won't know until he wakes up."

Tina looked down at the man who lay so silent and still on the table. His short, dark brown hair was disheveled and his face was pale and streaked with blood, but something about his features tugged at Tina. "He doesn't look like a criminal."

The doctor snorted. "Neither did Ted Bundy." His hands moved over the patient, gentle yet probing. "No matter who he is, he's one lucky guy. That cut on his head is going to need suturing and it feels like he might have a couple of broken ribs, but other than that and a concussion, he looks like he's going to be all right."

Tina pressed on the gauze pad she was holding over the wound on the man's head, holding it more firmly to slow the bleeding. "What do you want me to do?"

The doctor raked his gaze over the patient, giving him an assessing look that Tina recognized. Then he said, "Get him cleaned up so I can suture that cut. Our first priority is stopping that bleeding."

They worked in silence for the next half hour. The doctor occasionally muttered a request to Tina, but she usually anticipated his needs and handed him an instrument before he asked. When the doctor finally stepped back, there was a neat line of sutures along the left side of the stranger's head.

"Get that bandaged, then we'll get him into X ray and get a scan of his head and chest. I want to make sure there isn't any other damage."

Tina gently covered the wound with a bandage and

tape, then hovered over their unconscious patient, reluctant to leave him alone. "Is there anyone with him?"

"The paramedics told me he was alone in the car. I have no idea if the police have managed to locate his family." He looked around the emergency room, where the chaos that had reigned earlier was beginning to subside. "It looks like things have quieted down a little." He shook his head. "I don't think this is the way most of these people planned to spend their Halloween."

The doctor helped her load the man onto a gurney, then she wheeled him out of the emergency room and over to the X ray department. The technician glanced briefly down at the patient, then looked back at Tina. "Another one from the Steele ball?"

"Car accident," she said, handing him the papers the emergency room doctor had filled out. "He needs a scan of his head and chest."

The technician looked at the papers and frowned. "This doesn't have any insurance information. We need that before we can get started."

The flare of anger took Tina by surprise. "You know that's not true in an emergency," she said, her voice cold. "He was alone in the car and the police haven't brought his ID in yet. I'm sure you'll get the information as soon as it's available. But we need that scan now."

Tina stood in the waiting room while the technician performed the tests on her patient, pacing from one side to the other. "What's the matter with you?" she muttered to herself. "This guy is just another patient."

But he wasn't just another patient. For some reason, Tina felt unusually protective of the unnamed man. Maybe it was because he was completely helpless and alone, no one waiting anxiously for him in the waiting room, no one to hold his hand as he lay unconscious. Or maybe it was because of the doctor's quick, careless assumption that he was a criminal, involved with the man who had shot and killed David and Lisa Steele.

Or maybe it was because she found him attractive. She forced herself to face the truth. Even though a bandage covered half of his head, he was still a very handsome man. Thick eyelashes fanned out against his pale cheeks. His face was lean, but there were lines around his eyes that told her he smiled frequently. She wondered what color those eyes were, wondered if she would see kindness or indifference in them when he woke up.

It didn't matter, she told herself, appalled at the direction her thoughts were taking. She was a professional, dedicated to giving her patients the best care she possibly could. And as a professional, she didn't get involved with her patients, either.

Thank goodness she had remembered that, she told herself firmly.

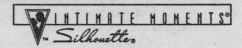

**INTIMATE MOMENTS®**
*Silhouette®*

presents a riveting 12-book continuity series:

*a Year of loving dangerously*

**Where passion rules and nothing is what it seems...**

When dishonor threatens a top-secret agency, the brave
men and women of SPEAR are prepared to risk it all as they
put their lives—and their hearts—on the line.

### Available October 2000:

# HER SECRET WEAPON
## by Beverly Barton

The only way agent Burke Lonigan can protect his pretty
assistant is to offer her the safety of his privileged lifestyle—as
his wife. But what will Burke do when he discovers Callie is
the same beguiling beauty he shared one forgotten night of
passion with—and the mother of his secret child?

*Available only from Silhouette Intimate Moments
at your favorite retail outlet.*

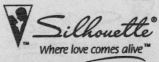

**Silhouette®**
*Where love comes alive™*

Coming Soon
Silhouette Books presents

*Weddings in White*

(on sale September 2000)

A 3-in-1 keepsake collection
by international bestselling author

# DIANA PALMER

Three heart-stoppingly handsome bachelors are paired
up with three innocent beauties who long to marry the
men of their dreams. This dazzling collection showcases
the enchanting characters and searing passion that
has made Diana Palmer a legendary talent
in the romance industry.

### *Unlikely Lover:*
Can a feisty secretary and a gruff oilman fight
the true course of love?

### *The Princess Bride:*
For better, for worse, starry-eyed Tiffany Blair captivated
Kingman Marshall's iron-clad heart....

### *Callaghan's Bride:*
Callaghan Hart swore marriage was for fools—until
Tess Brady branded him with her sweetly seductive kisses!

*Available at your favorite retail outlet.*

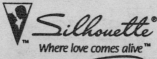

*Silhouette*®
*Where love comes alive*™

Visit Silhouette at www.eHarlequin.com

PSWIW

**Don't miss
an exciting opportunity
to save on the purchase of
Harlequin and Silhouette books!**

Buy any two Harlequin or
Silhouette books and save
**$10.00 off** future Harlequin
and Silhouette purchases

OR

buy any three
Harlequin or Silhouette books
and save **$20.00 off** future
Harlequin and Silhouette purchases.

**Watch for details
coming in October 2000!**

PHQ400

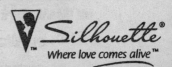

If you enjoyed what you just read,
then we've got an offer you can't resist!

# Take 2 bestselling
# love stories FREE!
# Plus get a FREE surprise gift!

**Clip this page and mail it to Silhouette Reader Service™**

| IN U.S.A. | IN CANADA |
| --- | --- |
| 3010 Walden Ave. | P.O. Box 609 |
| P.O. Box 1867 | Fort Erie, Ontario |
| Buffalo, N.Y. 14240-1867 | L2A 5X3 |

**YES!** Please send me 2 free Silhouette Intimate Moments® novels and my free surprise gift. Then send me 6 brand-new novels every month, which I will receive months before they're available in stores. In the U.S.A., bill me at the bargain price of $3.80 plus 25¢ delivery per book and applicable sales tax, if any*. In Canada, bill me at the bargain price of $4.21 plus 25¢ delivery per book and applicable taxes**. That's the complete price and a savings of at least 10% off the cover prices—what a great deal! I understand that accepting the 2 free books and gift places me under no obligation ever to buy any books. I can always return a shipment and cancel at any time. Even if I never buy another book from Silhouette, the 2 free books and gift are mine to keep forever. So why not take us up on our invitation. You'll be glad you did!

245 SEN C226
345 SEN C227

| Name | (PLEASE PRINT) | |
| --- | --- | --- |
| Address | Apt.# | |
| City | State/Prov. | Zip/Postal Code |

\* Terms and prices subject to change without notice. Sales tax applicable in N.Y.
\*\* Canadian residents will be charged applicable provincial taxes and GST.
 All orders subject to approval. Offer limited to one per household.
® are registered trademarks of Harlequin Enterprises Limited.

INMOM00                                    ©1998 Harlequin Enterprises Limited

# COMING NEXT MONTH